THE TEN LOVES OF MR NISHINO

Also by Hiromi Kawakami from Granta Books

*The Nakano Thrift Shop*
*Strange Weather in Tokyo*

# The Ten Loves
# of Mr Nishino

Hiromi Kawakami

*Translated from the Japanese
by Allison Markin Powell*

**GRANTA**

Granta Publications, 12 Addison Avenue, London W11 4QR

First published in Great Britain by Granta Books, 2019

Copyright © Hiromi Kawakami, 2003

English translation copyright © Allison Markin Powell, 2019

Originally published in Japan in 2003 under the title *Nishino Yukihiko no koi to boken* by Shinchosha, Tokyo.

The moral right of Hiromi Kawakami to be identified as the author of this work and of Allison Markin Powell to be identified as the translator of this work has been asserted by them in accordance with the Copyright, Designs and Patents Act 1988.

A CIP catalogue record for this book is available from the British Library

9 8 7 6 5 4 3 2 1

ISBN 978 1 84627 697 2
eISBN 978 1 84627 702 3

www.granta.com

Typeset by Avon DataSet, Bidford on Avon, Warwickshire

Printed and bound by CPI Group (UK) Ltd, Croydon, CR0 4YY

MIX
Paper from
responsible sources
FSC
www.fsc.org
FSC® C020471

# Contents

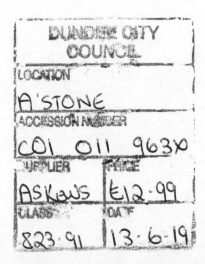

# Parfait

Minami was a shy child back then, only seven years old.

Always folding origami with her thin fingers. Morning glories. An organ. Parakeets. A little offering stand. She made all kinds of things, and then quietly put them away in a box covered with gaily patterned *Chiyogami* craft paper. I had been quite young when Minami was born.

When Minami was seven, I was still in my twenties, and sometimes I disliked her. My heart would ache after these unpleasant feelings, and I would hug Minami all the more tightly. It might have been my youth, coupled with the fact that Minami was still as tender and defenceless as a baby, which invited my dislike. Whenever I held Minami tight, she would always be very quiet and still. Minami didn't say much when she was little.

I was in love back then.

Whatever love is, anyway.

The person I was in love with was named Nishino – he was a full twelve years older. I slept with Nishino many times.

The first time Nishino put his arms around me, I silently let him hold me, the same way as Minami did with me, without wondering whether it was love or passion or whatever. Each time I saw Nishino, I would nestle in closer to him, but for Nishino the feeling was always the same, no matter what.

What is love, really? People have the right to fall in love, but not the right to be loved. I fell in love with Nishino, but that's not to say that he was then required to fall in love with me. I knew this, but what was so painful was that my feelings for Nishino had no effect on his feelings for me. Despite this pain, I longed for him more and more.

Nishino called the house once while my husband was home. My husband didn't say a word – he just handed me the receiver. Then he murmured, 'Someone from an insurance company.'

Taking the phone from my husband, I whispered succinct responses into the mouthpiece: 'Yes.' 'Right.' 'No.' 'Very well then.' I listened to Nishino's voice on the other end of the line, him pretending to speak in the tone of an insurance salesman, adding deliberate pauses as he said things like, 'I want to make love to you right now,' while I thought to myself, *I might not even like this person, really.*

My husband was at my side, quietly looking over some paperwork, when I took this call from Nishino. My husband may have known everything or nothing at all. During the three years or so from the time I first met Nishino and fell in love with him, to when he gradually began keeping his distance, to when finally even the phone calls stopped, my husband never asked me any questions.

Staring at the tidy nape of my husband's neck, I repeated the same words: 'Yes.' 'Right.' 'I see.' Nishino chatted for a few minutes and then abruptly hung up. Nishino was always the one to end our calls. I may not have liked him, but I was in love with Nishino.

Sometimes Minami came with me to see Nishino. He would request that I bring her along.

'Little girls are great,' he often said. Nishino was unmarried. He must have already been in his forties at that time. Even though he was seven years older than my husband, Nishino had none of the slightly detached self-possession of my spouse. Nishino always seemed uncomfortable around people, although he was apparently quite capable at his job – I remember being surprised, when we first met, by the impressive title on the business card he handed me.

Nishino would always have a small gift for Minami. 'Just open it,' Nishino would prompt her, and Minami would unwrap the package, without a word. The paper rustled as her slender fingers untied the red ribbon.

A delicate calligraphy brush stand encrusted with pink shells. A paperweight in the shape of a dog. A bean-paste bun sprinkled with poppy seeds. A music box no bigger than the palm of her hand. Minami gazed at these gifts, her expression barely registering any change, and then with a slight bow she would say softly, 'Thank you.'

From the beginning, Minami never asked anything about Nishino. She simply held my hand, quiet at my side like a shadow. Should I have worried that Minami would say something about Nishino to my husband? Did a part of me hope that she might accidentally let it slip to him?

When Minami came along with me, Nishino and I had no physical contact. Instead, we would go to a restaurant that had a terrace, and before Minami could say a word he would order her a strawberry parfait, and hot coffee for himself and me. If strawberries weren't in season, he ordered banana parfait.

'Chocolate parfait is no good!' Nishino would declare, drawing out the last syllable of 'parfait', so that it sounded like 'par-fay-ee'. Minami would nod vaguely, as would I.

As we nodded, I stole a glance at Minami, who was looking my way. Within the pale whites of her eyes, her pupils were starkly round and fixed on me. I raised my eyebrows slightly, and Minami smiled faintly, her brow lifting as well.

Minami never finished her parfait. And yet Nishino ordered strawberry or banana parfait every time.

'Minami, dear, will get a par-fay-ee, right?' he said, a slightly higher note than usual creeping into his voice as he peered at Minami's downcast face.

After we left the restaurant, the three of us would always make two trips along the path that ran through the park. Then we would head to the train station, where we'd part at the ticket gate. Nishino bought tickets for us. He would place them in our hands – an adult ticket for me and a child ticket for Minami.

Once our tickets were punched, I'd turn back to see Nishino grinning and waving at us from the other side of the ticket gate. Minami never looked back, she just headed straight for the stairs in front of us. Nishino still waved at Minami, who clearly had no intention of turning around. Nishino waved at me, he waved at Minami and he waved at the space in between us.

'Mr Nishino was a strange guy, wasn't he, Mum?' Minami said to me the spring she turned fifteen.

The last time I saw Nishino, it had been winter. Minami was ten years old when he and I broke up. At the time, I hadn't explained to Minami that Nishino and I wouldn't be seeing each other any more, and she hadn't mentioned him at all since then.

Now that I thought about it, while I was still involved with Nishino, there had been a few times when Minami had even laughed out loud in his presence. Once she realized that I was staring at her as she laughed, she had stopped, seemingly self-conscious. And then she had sneezed softly several times.

By that spring, when Minami turned fifteen, I hardly ever thought about Nishino any more. The sound of Nishino's name suddenly emerging from Minami's lips triggered a range of emotions within me. It felt as though a hole had been pricked in my belly and air was now leaking out.

'Mum, you and Mr Nishino were lovers, weren't you?' Minami asked, looking me straight in the eye.

I thought about it, but I no longer knew. Even when Nishino and I had been seeing each other frequently, I hadn't been sure. I no longer knew whether Nishino and I had been in love, or whether I had really liked him, or even whether or not someone named Nishino had ever actually existed.

'When he called me "Minami, dear", it felt as if the palm of my hand had thick paint on it that I couldn't wash off, no matter how hard I tried,' Minami murmured softly, as though she was singing.

For the past year or so, Minami had been having a growth spurt. Her arms and legs kept getting longer and longer. Minami seemed to be made up of entirely new cells – as if her metabolism was so high that every few days the cells in her body were replaced completely.

'The problem with Mr Nishino was, after seeing him, there was always some trace that seemed to linger.'

'A trace?'

'A sort of melancholy trace of something, almost bittersweet.'

'Minami, why don't we go get a par-fay-ee, for old times' sake?' I suggested, imitating the way that Nishino used to draw out the last syllable.

Minami laughed. 'I wonder how Mr Nishino's doing.'

'I'm sure he's just fine.'

'I love the dog paperweight.'

Long after Nishino and I broke up, Minami still cherished the silver dog paperweight that Nishino had given her. She had named him Koro, and every so often she gave him a good shine with polishing sand.

'And the bean-paste bun with poppy seeds, that was delicious.'

Nishino had a knack for giving gifts. To me too, though he had only given me a present once. A small silver bell.

Dangling from my hand, it produced a clear ring.

'From now on, I want you to wear it,' Nishino had said with a smile. 'Then I'll always know where you are, Natsumi.'

'And once you know, what will you do?' I must have said. 'Will you run away, like the mice who belled the cat?'

'No, it's so that I can catch you, Natsumi – so you won't run away. As long as I know your whereabouts, then you can't leave me.'

Nishino's words had made me blush a little.

The next time I saw Nishino, I wore the bell on a chain around my wrist. While he made love to me, the bell tinkled faintly the entire time. 'I'm not letting you go,' Nishino said.

I wonder what happened to that little bell. When I think of Nishino's embrace, I am struck with a fleeting wistfulness, but I cannot quite recall in which way I had been in love with him.

I told Minami, 'Nishino said that when you grow up he'd like to go on a date with you.'

'Very funny!' Minami cried out.

'That's the kind of guy he was.'

'A perv, you mean?'

'He was just overindulged.'

'He was ridiculous.' But Minami's voice was tender when she said this. She may not even have noticed the sweetness in her voice.

'Minami, is there someone you like?'

'Nope,' she answered reflexively and stood up, an

expression of denial on her face. With long strides she took
the stairs, two at a time, and slammed the door to her room.

I wondered what Nishino had seemed like to Minami
back then. As she had ascended the stairs, Minami's body
had emitted that saccharine scent that was particular to a
girl her age. For the first time in a while, I had the urge to
hear Nishino's voice. This feeling that the fifteen-year-old
Minami had evoked in me was different from the dislike
she had aroused when she was seven years old, but it was
still unpleasant.

Minami is now twenty-five.

She must have had a number of romances. Yet Minami
has never said a word about any of them to me. Just as, when
she was little, she quietly went about folding her origami, she
must have quietly fallen in and out of love.

It's been fifteen years or so since Nishino and I broke
up. And it's only now, after all that time has passed, that I've
finally been able to remember him clearly.

Quite often, I am struck by a memory of his voice or
his body, or of something he said. As often as I am aware
of someone who is right there. It happens so frequently, it
has occurred to me that Nishino might not even be around
any more.

Come to think of it, 'When I die' was the kind of thing
Nishino would just come out with. He would say it in a
slightly indulgent tone. Sometimes I'm surprised when I
realize that Minami is now practically the same age I was
when I was seeing Nishino.

Long ago, Nishino would say, 'The truth is, I want to get married.'

I would reply, 'If you want to, why don't you?'

'Would you marry me, Natsumi?' Nishino would ask.

Knowing that he wasn't serious, I would always shake my head.

'C'mon, you're no fun!' Nishino would say cheerily, and I would feel a tightening in my chest. I pretended not to notice, but back when I was seeing Nishino, the plentiful shadows of other women were always lurking. This was what enabled him to speak so cruelly of marriage to me.

'Hey, Natsumi, when I die, I'll come to you,' he once said.

'What?'

'When I die, I want to be by your side.'

'I bet you say that to all the girls,' I replied flippantly.

With an unusually serious look, Nishino said, 'I don't.'

'Mum, someone's in the garden,' Minami called out.

Today was Friday, but Minami had taken a day off and had been at the house since the morning. Every so often, Minami would take days off from work for no reason. 'What's the matter?' I would ask, and she would simply smile at me, without saying a word.

I had a hunch it was Nishino.

I had just started to simmer some pumpkin, and the aroma of the mildly sweet stock wafted throughout the kitchen. The old refrigerator hummed noisily.

I stayed where I was, standing in front of the sink. 'Minami, see who it is,' I said.

The slatted door to the garden opened. A moment later, I heard the clatter of wooden sandals on the paving stones. Soon the sound of her steps stopped. A gust of wind came up, and the grass rustled.

Then all sound ceased.

'Mum, come here,' Minami called from the garden.

Just as Minami's voice rang out, the refrigerator started humming again.

'I'm not coming out,' I replied slowly through the kitchen window.

I looked out at the garden through the lattice.

The shape of someone who seemed like Nishino was sitting in the dense weeds.

Through his shadow, his surroundings were clearly visible. He sat amid the thick grass, almost blending in with it. Minami was squatting, as she peered into the face of whoever this was.

He sat upright and tall. When Nishino was alive, he had been a bit more restless. He always seemed as though he wasn't quite used to the air around him – he would be blinking his eyes or brushing back his hair.

'Water . . .' Minami was asking. 'Would you like some?'

The shadow nodded slightly.

Even though Minami and the shadow of Nishino were some distance from where I stood in the kitchen, somehow I could clearly make out both of their movements.

I turned on the tap and filled a delicate glass with water. Then I made my way as far as the door, being careful as I walked not to spill a drop.

Minami was waiting there for me, standing on the paving stones.

\*

'What is that?' Minami asked.

'Don't you know?' I replied in a low voice.

'Is it Mr Nishino?'

'It must be.'

'Is he dead?'

'Yes, probably.'

Minami and I looked at each other calmly. The wind chimes jingled. In the grass, Nishino stirred.

'Is it all right if you're not the one to give it to him?' Minami asked as she took the glass of water from me.

'I'd like you to give it to him for me.'

'But . . .'

'You give it to him.'

Minami pursed her lips, turning down the corners of her mouth and, with a sort of reckless gait, walked back to where Nishino was. The water in the glass formed ripples, spilling over a bit. She passed the glass to Nishino and squatted beside him. Nishino accepted the glass politely with both hands and carefully drank all of the water.

'He'd like more.' As she handed me the empty glass, Minami seemed to be glaring. 'Mum, why don't you bring it to him?'

Small dragonflies were flitting through the grass. They darted among the foxtails and smartweed. Nishino sat there, looking in my direction. His mouth was moving, but I couldn't hear what he was saying. I went to the kitchen to fill the glass again.

'Mum, why is Mr Nishino here?' Minami asked. I remained silent, and just shook my head.

After draining the second glass of water, Nishino lay down on the ground. Minami took an old deckchair out of the shed and placed it next to him, kicking off her sandals as she sat down. Occasionally she and Nishino would exchange a few words.

'I asked him why he's here, but he won't answer,' Minami said from the deckchair with a sigh, turning her head towards me.

'He told me he would come,' I replied lightly, sitting on the veranda.

Nishino's eyes were closed as he lay there, and he was humming. The longing that I had once felt for him came back to me vividly. Nishino had a lot of grey hair at his temples, and there were wrinkles around his eyes and mouth. It was the face of a man long past fifty.

'Nishino,' I called out for the first time.

Nishino kept humming. It sounded like the folk song 'Song of the Seashore'. Next to him, Minami chanted, 'If I wandered along the seashore tomorrow ...'

From the veranda where I sat, I joined in softly.

*If I wandered along the seashore tomorrow, I would remember things from long ago.*

'Nishino, this song is a little too appropriate for you,' I called out, this time trying to sound as cheerful as possible.

Nishino sat up slowly. 'He-heh-heh,' he chuckled.


'Natsumi, I'm here,' Nishino spoke in a clear voice as he beckoned me.

'Yes, here you are,' I said, ignoring his gesture and

standing up on the spot where I was.

'Because I promised. I promised you, Natsumi, didn't I?'

Nishino sounded just like himself. His voice had that distinctive slightly indulgent tone.

Minami wore an expression of astonishment as she sat in the deckchair, hugging her knees.

'Did you ever have a daughter?' I asked from afar.

'I never married.'

There were plenty of dragonflies and butterflies darting about now. Some of them even alighted on Minami's shoulders or arms. A light breeze stirred the wind chimes.

'Minami, dear, you're so pretty now.' Nishino's eyes squinted with affection. 'I wasn't able to fulfil my promise to take you out on a date.'

'I never made that promise!' Minami pouted her lips.

'I wouldn't have taken you out for a par-fay-ee. It would have been a more grown-up date.' As always, he drew out the word 'par-fay-ee'.

'Mr Nishino, I never liked parfait,' Minami said mischievously.

'I knew that.' Nishino reached out a hand and gently patted Minami's bare arm. The dragonflies and butterflies that had alighted on her all dispersed at once.

'Nishino.' I called out his name softly, and he sat up straight again, holding his hand out towards me.

'Come, Natsumi.' He looked at me with puppy-dog eyes.

'No, I'm fine here. I don't need to come over to where you are,' I replied quietly.

'Come here, Natsumi. I'm lonely.'

'I'm lonely too.'

'Minami, dear, you don't look like your mother. You're very pretty, Minami, dear, but your mother, Natsumi, is a beauty,' Nishino said, his tone shifting.

That was just like Nishino. Minami laughed to herself. 'I have my father's eyes, my mother's nose and my grandma's mouth,' Minami recited in a murmur.

'Mum, stop wasting time in there and come here – no doubt Mr Nishino will be gone soon enough.'

The lush hydrangea leaves seemed to rustle in concert with Minami's voice. Barefoot, I stepped into the garden. Pebbles stuck to the soles of my feet. The seeds on the wild grasses grazed my calves.

'Is your husband well?' Nishino asked, sitting with his heels tucked neatly under him.

'Every day is peaceful and quiet.'

'What more can one ask for?' As Nishino spoke these words, Minami sneezed.

'He comes all the way here after he died and the two of you are making small talk?' she said as she continued to sneeze three times in a row.

'Thank you for coming,' I said as I approached Nishino, and rubbed my cheek against his.

'A promise is a promise!'

'I didn't know you were so conscientious.'

'Not when it comes to my body, but always when it comes to my heart.'

'You haven't changed a bit, have you?' I said, pecking him on the cheek. Nishino looked as if he might cry, but he didn't.

'I'd like to be buried in this garden,' Nishino said sincerely.

'No way,' Minami murmured with a smile.

'She's right – no way,' I agreed.

*That's enough, Nishino*, I said inside my head. *I'm just happy you're here.*

'Well, then, at least make me a grave.' Nishino's tone sounded just like when he used to order a parfait, all those years ago.

'A grave?' Minami retorted with surprise.

'Like one for a goldfish. That would be nice.'

I looked at Nishino's face. His expression was the one he'd often worn when he was alive, like that of a child being scolded by his mother.

'All right,' I replied, and Nishino took me gently in his arms.


Nishino stayed in the garden until just before the sun set.

I went back to the kitchen and fried up dinner. Minami remained by Nishino's side the whole time. As I was disposing of the cooking oil, I heard Minami cry out.

*He must have left*, I thought.

A moment later, Minami appeared in the kitchen, her gaze fixed on the floor as she murmured, 'He's gone.'

*Yes, he's gone*, I said to myself. I searched for a set of pincers at the back of a drawer. I pulled out a big wooden box filled with smaller boxes of somen noodles, selected one of the smaller boxes and used the pincers to remove the nails at the four corners. I took apart the box and set the littlest rectangular piece of wood on the counter. I went to get the calligraphy set that Minami had used in middle school and, on top of the counter, I ground the ink. Then with a thick brush I wrote out, 'Here lies Nishino.'

I went out into the garden and, beside the graves of our goldfish and cat, I thrust the wood into the ground.

'Back then, I really did love you, Nishino,' I said like a prayer, my palms held together as I crouched before the grave. Minami squatted next to me.

We remained still, our eyes closed and hands in prayer. Then we both looked at each other.

'Sometime, let's go out for a par-fay-ee,' I said to Minami as I stood up slowly. Minami nodded, without a word.

The dragonflies and the butterflies had also left the garden. Far in the distance, I could hear the tinkling of a bell.

# In the Grass

I buried fourteen candles.

With a small shovel that was starting to rust, I dug up the moist earth.

At the back of the vacant lot, about thirty steps from the way in, past the overgrown weeds – in summer they got as tall as me – there were several trees. A magnolia. A camphor too. Those are the only two kinds of trees that I know. The branches of the rest of the trees in the cluster – whatever kind they were – stretched towards the sky, and in autumn they dropped little acorns.

The weeds thinned out a bit under the trees. I used the shovel to dig up the earth in this spot, where the weeds were sparse. By the roots of the camphor tree, I laid the fourteen short, thin candles in a hole about ten centimetres deep. I covered the candles with the earth I had dug up. Once the candles were no longer visible, I carefully levelled off the ground, then I stamped on it with the bottom of my shoe.

I continued to trample upon the ground until no one

could tell that the candles were buried there or even that a hole had been dug. I stepped back a little and looked at the trodden earth. The slightly uneven surface of the ground.

'Hmph,' I muttered, grabbing my school bag, which I had left in the weeds. I put the shovel in a plastic bag and shoved it into my school bag. I pushed my way roughly through the weeds and left the vacant lot. I could hear the sound of autumn insects here and there. I walked straight home.

I turned fourteen yesterday. The candles had been on my birthday cake. Last night, I had blown them out with one breath. At the same moment I blew them out, my father had clapped his hands. Then my father and I cut up the cake and ate it in silence. We stuffed our faces with buttercream rose petals.

When I did speak – to say 'Tastes good' – my father raised the corners of his mouth and nodded. But the truth was, it wasn't any good at all.

This was the fifth time just the two of us were celebrating my birthday. My mother left home the week before I turned ten. The following week, I celebrated my birthday, just my father and me for the first time. The cake my father bought was sort of crude, compared to the one my mother had always got for me. The birthday cake my mother bought was a softer sponge cake, heaped with fresh whipped cream and sprinkled with chocolate. The number of candles on it then was not my age but for some reason, always precisely three. She made a special trip on the train to a pastry shop on a big shopping street, to pick up the cake, which she'd ordered in advance.

My father didn't try to explain why my mother had left. He hadn't spoken a word about my mother since. But one day my aunt Namiko, my father's sister, let something slip, so I knew that apparently my mother had run off with some other man.

Of course, I never said anything to my father about the fact that I knew my mother had run off with someone else. As far as I was concerned – and my father as well – she did not exist. From that day forward. And forever after.


I had known about the vacant lot for a long time. During the summer holidays when I was in year one and two, the boys would get up early in the morning and go there to catch the stag beetles that gathered on the trees at the back of the lot. I'd be right there with them, catching those little creatures with what looked like antlers on their heads. In those days, there were quite a number of vacant lots around my house – the lot where I buried the candles was just one of many.

Over the past several years, the vacant lots have dwindled as new homes were steadily built. The number of stag beetles and rhinoceros beetles has also dropped considerably. Now that lot is about the only space left that's as wide open as this.

Soon after I started middle school, it became my habit to stop at the lot on my way home. I rarely saw anyone else there. I guess not even the primary school kids played here any more. It was just a deserted tract of land with the occasional leaping grasshopper.

*

The first thing I buried in the vacant lot was my goldfish Tara.

I had kept Tara in a bowl by the front door. The bowl had previously been home to two goldfish I had got at a Shinto festival.

One was a pop-eyed goldfish, the other was a red goldfish, and I had scooped them both up from a night-stall vendor. I carried the plastic bag that held both fish, and on the way home we stopped at a tropical fish shop where my mother bought me a round fishbowl. The edge had a wavy shape, and the glass was a very pale blue.

The goldfish from the festival were named A-suke and B-maru, and I fed them every day. A-suke was the pop-eyed one, and B-maru was the red one. My mother and I came up with their names.

However, A-suke and B-maru had short lives. It may be that I overfed them. Or perhaps in the night-stall vendor's water tank they were already in poor health. Three days after bringing them home, A-suke was floating belly-up in the bowl, followed the very next day by B-maru.

Those third and fourth nights, I cried and wailed. On the morning of the fifth day, my eyes were so swollen my father took one look at me and said, 'Shiori, your face – it looks like the goldfish put a curse on you.'

'You're so stupid, Dad!' I yelled, and my mother gave me a stern warning.

'What kind of behaviour is this, calling a parent stupid?' she had said.

\*

When I came home from school that day, there had been a goldfish – bigger than both A-suke and B-maru had been – swimming around in the bowl by the front door.

I flew into the kitchen to ask my mother about it. 'What's with the fish by the front door?'

'I bought it at the tropical fish shop,' she answered logically.

Had I asked my father, no doubt his reply would have been something like, 'A-suke and B-maru loved you so much, Shiori, that they united in heaven and came back.'

'Will this one last very long?' I wondered.

My mother thought for a moment. 'I don't know, but I asked the man at the shop to select a fish as strong and healthy as possible, so I think it may live a long life – but there's no way to be sure.'

'I hope it lives a long life,' I said, and my mother nodded.

Because the fish was red and about the size of a *tarako* cod roe, my mother named it Tara.

Tara died the year after my mother left. It had been just over two years since she brought it home. I didn't like the idea of burying Tara in the garden, so I brought it to the vacant lot, and buried it there. With the same shovel I would use for the candles, I buried Tara near the entrance to the lot.

It was towards the end of autumn, so the weeds had grown sparse. As I shovelled, alone, I murmured over and over, 'I pray for the soul of Tara.' I hated saying the name Tara. It reminded me of my mother. But it wasn't Tara's fault that it had that name.

I didn't know whether or not just over two years was a long life for a goldfish.

*

Since Tara, I've buried numerous things in the vacant lot.

Eleven candles. A toy ring. The boxwood comb from my mother's chest of drawers. Twelve candles. Painkiller tablets. Thirteen candles. A frog figurine. A chipped mug.

Some things were connected to my mother, some weren't. I remember where I buried each and every one of them.

The week after I buried the fourteen candles, I got a letter.

When I opened the shoe cupboard at the end of the school day, there was a white rectangular envelope inside. It was not an envelope that I or the other girls in my class usually used – not one of those made of paper that was crisp to the touch, in shades of tea, grass and peach – this was a business envelope, the kind an adult would use.

On the front of it, 'Ms Shiori Yamagata' was written vertically in black felt-tip pen.

I turned it over and saw the name 'Toru Tanabe'.

I didn't recognize this name or the handwriting. I mean, the only handwriting I was familiar with was that of the teachers and the characters they'd write on the blackboard, and the scrawls of Toko and Chie in the notebooks that we lent to and borrowed from each other. The characters that spelled out 'Ms Shiori Yamagata' were large and vigorous.

I put the letter in my bag and went to the vacant lot.

Even though summer was long gone, the lot was still overgrown with weeds. I sat down on the rock that had always been beside the magnolia tree and opened the letter.

*Ms Shiori Yamagata,*

*Please forgive me for writing this letter out of the blue.*

*My name is Toru Tanabe. I'm a year-nine student in room C.*

*You and I have never been in the same class together, but I noticed you just after the matriculation ceremony.*

*Would you like to see a movie together sometime soon?*

*I'm in the Science Club.*

*My hobby is wireless radios.*

*I thought you might be surprised if I suddenly asked you out, so I wrote you a letter first.*

*If it's all right, I'll ask you out the next time I see you.*

*Sincerely,*

*Toru Tanabe*

The opening 'Ms Shiori Yamagata' and the closing 'Toru Tanabe' were written in blue ink; the rest of the lines were in black. I read the letter over three times. I wondered whether he had added the names in blue after writing it.

I wasn't the type of girl who was enormously popular with the boys. Not like Chie, for instance, who had a new boyfriend every few weeks, or like Toko, who had Kitabayashi and was always getting a lift home from school with him, riding double on his bicycle. I had gone out with boys before – to an amusement park or to the movies – but none of these dates had ever amounted to any kind of serious relationship. We would go out once or twice, and that would be the end of it.

I knew I could be a bit brusque. The truth was, I didn't

really get what was so fun about hanging out with boys. Chie, with her constant rotation – that kind of thing I could understand – but Toko, who had decided on the one guy, Kitabayashi, and spent all her time with him – that was a mystery to me.

'You'll understand, Shiori, once you find a guy you're crazy about,' Toko had said.

'Do you really think so?' I'd replied, but somehow I had the feeling that I would never be like her.

I could imagine Toko's life story – she would fall perfectly in love with a guy, marry him, have children, then they would have her grandchildren and eventually she would die peacefully, surrounded by those children and grandchildren. My life story would probably play out quite a bit differently. The man I loved and children too might very well appear at some point, but their arrival would perhaps be strange and unexpected, and then again, they might never materialize at all.

'You're only in year nine, Shiori – how can you go on about these things?' Toko had laughed.

'You know, we're not as simple as you think, Shiori,' Chie had said, slightly miffed.

I neatly refolded the letter from Toru Tanabe and put it back in the white rectangular envelope. I liked Toru Tanabe's letter, quite a lot. If he did invite me out, I knew that I would nod to him in acceptance. Although I couldn't be bothered to think about what would come after that.

We'd probably hang out once or twice – see a movie, have tea together, go to an arcade. We might take a leisurely walk along the river or on some pleasant street. But that would be the end of it.

As for Toru Tanabe, and other boys I hadn't yet met, they still weren't any more distinct to me than all of the grasses growing here in the vacant lot. I let out a sigh, and stood up to leave.

I saw Nishino in the vacant lot the day after I went to the movies with Toru Tanabe, which was a Monday.

Nishino and I had been in the same class since our first year in middle school. He didn't really stand out. He was about average height; his marks were about average too. For sports, I think he played tennis, or maybe baseball. I don't remember exactly.

Just once, Nishino and I had embraced. It wasn't as though we embraced because we loved each other – no, not like that. We were preparing for the school culture festival, and a ladder fell in my direction, but Nishino was able to brace it with his back – and in that instant, we ended up in each other's arms. Everyone in the class cheered, though that's all there was to it. Nishino's breath was warm, and I didn't find it unpleasant to be held by him. But it was only a moment.

Now Nishino was sitting on the rock – my rock – beside the magnolia tree, with a woman. Not a girl, but a woman. A pale woman with short hair.

I let out a little cry. Not because Nishino was sitting in my spot, or because he was there with a woman.

It was because the woman next to Nishino looked exactly like my mother.

\*

Hearing the sound of my cry, both Nishino and the woman slowly turned their heads. Their motions were perfectly in sync. It was as if a single puppet master were manipulating the movements of two dolls.

Now that she was turned towards me, the woman's face looked nothing like my mother's.

'Oh, Yamagata,' Nishino said. His voice did not sound all that surprised.

The woman smiled in my direction and then turned back to Nishino. 'A friend of yours?' she asked.

'A girl from my class,' Nishino replied curtly.

It was true that I was a girl from his class, yet I felt slightly miffed. Surely there was another way of saying it, wasn't there? He had barged into *my* vacant lot, and he was just going to dismiss me as 'a girl from his class'?

'What are you doing here?' I asked as coolly as I could manage.

'Nothing much,' Nishino said, standing up. The woman stood, following suit. As before, when they had both turned towards me, their movements were beautifully in sync with one another.

'I'm leaving,' the woman said softly, with a gentle touch of her fingers on Nishino's shoulder. The gesture was so light, I couldn't tell whether she actually touched him or not. Yet, to my eye, the movement of the woman's fingers appeared to blaze a pure white trail in the air. The trail went beyond Nishino's shoulder and left a distinct after-image.

'See you later.' She turned nimbly, and left.

Nishino and I stood where we were, watching her go.

*

'Nishino, do you live around here?' I asked.

Nishino hadn't moved from where he stood, so I stayed in place too. We had been standing there for several minutes in silence – or maybe it was only a few seconds, I really couldn't tell.

'No.' Nishino's reply was short. His voice sounded rather grown-up. It was completely different from that of other boys like Toru Tanabe. I must have heard Nishino's voice in class before, though I didn't have a clear recollection of what it might have sounded like. But this was definitely the first time I had heard this tone in his voice.

'Do you . . . come here a lot?'

Nishino offered no reply. He wasn't avoiding the question – it seemed more likely my words hadn't reached his ears. I strode over to my rock beside the magnolia tree where Nishino and the woman had been sitting, and with a certain roughness reclaimed my place. Nishino was watching my movements vacantly.

'Yamagata, you live round here?' Nishino asked after a while. His voice was different now. The voice he had been using until just a few moments ago was gone. He sounded like a totally normal year-nine boy, half child and half adult, uncertain, in the midst of breaking through adolescence.

'Just down the road,' I answered.

Nishino sat down in the weeds. The foxtails yielded, pinned under Nishino, right about where I had buried the boxwood comb.

I felt a shiver. Within the darkness beneath Nishino lay

the rotting boxwood comb. The feeling was unlike fear, or pleasure, or disgust, or sadness. Various things came together and mingled in the shiver that went through me.

A dragonfly flitted through the air. As I watched, it multiplied into several dragonflies, and then they disappeared, only to multiply again.

'I'm leaving,' Nishino said suddenly and stood up. Several small seeds from the grass were stuck to the trousers of his school uniform.

'Goodbye,' I said, still sitting on my rock.

'Goodbye,' Nishino said.

Nishino left, the grass seeds still attached to his trousers.


The next day, I saw Nishino in class, but neither one of us made eye contact. We didn't speak to each other either. At that point, I had barely ever spoken to Nishino in the classroom before.

Come to think of it, before Toko started going out with Kitabayashi, she'd actually had a little crush on Nishino. She was always keen to talk about him. Nishino, for his part, seemed uninterested in Toko. Chie used to tease Toko, saying, 'What do you see in that guy, Nishino?' But I thought I detected a note of bitterness in Chie's voice. I sometimes wondered if Chie may have also had a thing for Nishino, but of course I never brought it up.

Before long, Toko got together with Kitabayashi, and Nishino was no longer a topic of conversation.

That day, I followed Nishino's movements out of the corner of my eye. Nishino hardly talked at all. Even when he was within a scrum of boys who were all chatting away, all he ever contributed was the occasional response: 'Yeah' or 'No' or 'Uh-huh'. He never initiated anything. He would laugh along with everyone else, and if anyone asked him something, he would answer with a minimum of words.

But oddly, despite his reticence, Nishino did not come across as unsociable. With just a simple nod, he managed to give the impression to whoever he was talking to that he had actually responded at length.

A strange air drifted about Nishino. An air that none of the other kids in class had. I had the impression that, if I were to try to push that air around, there would be no end to it. The more I tried to push it, the deeper I would get caught up in it. And no matter how hard I pushed, I still would never reach Nishino on the other side. Nevertheless, there was something gentle and warm and pleasant about that air. And imperceptibly, it seemed to create the illusion that the air itself was Nishino, instead of the person.


Toru Tanabe and I were on our third film appreciation date. 'Film appreciation' was what Toru Tanabe had decided to call it. I did not dislike the phrase.

The first time I went out with Toru Tanabe, we saw a movie and went to a coffee shop, where we drank juice. Then we stopped at a bookshop, where Toru Tanabe showed me the wireless radio magazine that he bought each month, before going home. The second time, we saw a movie and drank coffee at the coffee shop, and then we stopped at the model train shop, where Toru Tanabe showed me the model train set that he was hoping to assemble. Toru Tanabe said he was an 'HO scaler', but I had no idea what he was talking about. The third time was also a film appreciation date, as Toru Tanabe had dubbed it.

'Girls usually find boys like me boring,'Toru Tanabe had said the second time we went out.

'Really?' I replied – I didn't think he was boring at all.

'Seems like it to me,' Toru Tanabe answered, giving the backpack over his shoulder a jolt. He was always carrying a large brown backpack. It was heavy. Once I had held it for him, and had been surprised by how heavy it was.

Toru Tanabe did not have the same air as Nishino. The air around Toru Tanabe was like that of a clear, fresh morning in the highlands.

'Wireless devices must be expensive?' I asked on our second date.

'They are,'Toru Tanabe confirmed.

'It's nice of your family to buy them for you,' I said.

Toru Tanabe smiled. 'I get my older brother's cast-offs,' he explained.

Toru Tanabe's older brother was at university, studying for a Masters degree in architecture. 'Yamagata, what do you want to do when you grow up?' Toru Tanabe asked. I thought about it for a moment, but absolutely nothing came to mind. I couldn't think of a single thing I wanted to do, nor wanted to be.

I had fallen silent. Toru Tanabe stared at me and scratched the top of his head.

'I always ask this question right away, and that must be why they say I'm boring.' Toru Tanabe looked down at me – he was a whole head taller.

'No, that's not why. It's just that I can't think of anything,' I replied.

Toru Tanabe squinted. 'Yamagata, you're really nice,' he said, and then he blushed.

Toru Tanabe had got it wrong. I really just couldn't think of anything. Absolutely nothing that I wanted to do. There were plenty of things that I didn't want to do. Like torment animals. Or be jealous of other people's happiness. Or cut my hair short. Or obey unreasonable orders. Or wear pastel-coloured dresses. The list went on and on.


After we had conducted our third film appreciation and gone again to the coffee shop, where we drank tea, instead of stopping at the bookshop or the model train shop, Toru Tanabe and I went to a park. He whistled as we walked around the park. I had to walk briskly to match his pace. His legs were longer than mine, and he was a fast walker.

When we arrived at the fountain, Toru Tanabe stopped whistling. There was a small grove of trees by the side of the fountain. Toru Tanabe walked in front of me and started to head into the trees. I broke into a trot to keep up with him.

Once we got to a spot where we were sort of hidden, Toru Tanabe came suddenly to a halt. Since I had been running, I almost collided with him from behind. He spun around and looked down at my face. There were faint beads of sweat on his forehead.

'Can I kiss you?' Toru Tanabe asked.

I said yes – it wasn't as if I hadn't expected it. In fact,

I had, and yet I didn't know what to do now. I didn't know whether I wanted to kiss Toru Tanabe or not. When I didn't say anything more, he stooped down and lifted my chin with his hand.

'No,' I said reflexively.

In that instant, Toru Tanabe let go of my chin and said softly, 'Sorry.'

'No, I'm the one who's sorry,' I replied, hastily turning my face towards him. I closed my eyes and waited for Toru Tanabe's kiss.

But his kiss never came. Through half-closed eyes, I peeked at him. Toru Tanabe was looking off towards the fountain.

'Sorry,' I repeated, opening my eyes.

'You don't have to say you're sorry,' Toru Tanabe said, and he patted me on the shoulder.

'Maybe it was too soon,' Toru Tanabe said after we had emerged from the trees. Then, with a troubled look, he gave a little laugh.

'No, that's not why,' I replied, my face serious, and soon the two of us were laughing together.

'It might have been a little early,' I said, still laughing.

We walked home along the path through the park, side by side.

'Can I hold your hand?' Toru Tanabe asked, and I nodded. He slowed his pace. Now I didn't have to hurry.

Toru Tanabe saw me to the front door of my house. 'Goodbye. See you later,' I said.

Toru Tanabe smiled. 'See you later,' he said.

I stood by the gate and watched his figure retreat, wondering to myself if I liked Toru Tanabe. I did like him. But whether I would learn to like kissing Toru Tanabe, that I didn't know.

I sort of felt like crying. I remembered the list of things I didn't want to do, from when Toru Tanabe had asked me about what I wanted to do in the future.

I didn't want to grow up. More than anything else, I was afraid of growing up and, without even knowing it, becoming exactly like my mother.

For the first time in a while, the day after my third date with Toru Tanabe, I went to the vacant lot.

I had kept my distance from it, ever since I happened to see Nishino and the woman there. I may not have admitted to myself that I didn't want to see the place where they were together, but I was well enough aware that there was something in the depths of my mind that kept me away.

The weeds were a little sparser. It was almost the middle of autumn. The leaves hadn't yet begun to change colour, but there were lots of acorns on the ground. The dragonflies were gone and there was only the faint chirping of insects in the grass.

Walking past my seat on the rock beside the magnolia tree, I went further in, where even more acorns had fallen, and sat down on a tree stump. The frog figurine was buried near its roots. My mother had had that frog figurine since before she was married. She had told me at some point, secretly, that an old boyfriend had given it to her. The frog figurine was made of striped agate and fitted in the palm of my hand.

Sometime after my mother left, my father got rid of my mother's belongings, but still, every so often things of hers would appear in unexpected places. The frog figurine had been hidden at the back of a shelf filled with albums. When I found the frog, I placed it in my palm. The striped agate felt cool to the touch. I had gone straight to the vacant lot, and buried it carefully.

I sat on the tree stump and waited. Somehow, I had the feeling that Nishino would show up. I was sure that Nishino, since seeing me here, had been to the lot several times with that woman. I knew that it probably made no difference to the two of them whether I was here or not. No one needed to tell me – it had been obvious from the way they had been when I saw them.

After a little while, Nishino and the woman arrived. Quietly, they sat down on the rock beside the magnolia tree. I held my breath and watched them.

The two of them were saying something and looking into each other's eyes. It didn't seem as though what they were saying was deeply meaningful or anything. But the two of them did not need to use words. With the sound of a mere sigh, they could communicate all they needed to say.

The insects were buzzing. I had turned into one of the grasses growing in the vacant lot. One of the grasses swaying in the gentle breeze, just listening to the sounds that filled the air.

The woman made a slight movement and touched Nishino's arm. As before, her gesture appeared to blaze a pure white trail in the air. A single line, drawn amid the grass. The woman guided Nishino's arm to the fabric of her blouse. Nishino allowed her to do this, and then he began to undo the buttons on her blouse, one at a time from the top. Her white bra became visible. Her breasts were large and round. These ample breasts seemed to contrast with the desolation in her face.

'Will you?' I thought I heard the woman say, but it may have been my imagination. Nishino unhooked the woman's bra. The moment he did so, the woman's breasts filled the air around her. They spilled over into it.

'They hurt,' the woman said. This time, I heard her clearly.

With her own finger, the woman pressed lightly on a nipple and a white liquid spurted out. Nishino was staring quietly. The woman pressed on her nipples several more times. Sprays of white soared through the air, like water gushing from a tap.

'They hurt. Please,' the woman said.

Slowly, Nishino bent down and brought his lips to the woman's breast. Nishino drew in his cheeks and suckled intently. His profile was beautiful. Even more than usual, his face looked like that of a child. *This is how an infant suckles*, I thought to myself. The woman's eyes were closed. Her face was expressionless; she just closed her eyes.

Once Nishino had finished one breast, he brought his face to the other. When he had finished with that one, Nishino pulled his face away and asked the woman, 'Better?'

'Thank you,' the woman said. Then she stood up rather casually, and left.

Nishino did not go after the woman. He remained seated on the rock beside the magnolia tree. I too sat very still on the tree stump. The sun began to set, and dusk fell around us. The next thing I knew, my cheeks were wet with tears.

I was shivering. This shiver was different from the one I had felt when Nishino was sitting on the spot where I had buried the boxwood comb.

It was beautiful. The sight of Nishino's face at the woman's breast, as he suckled intently – that had been quite beautiful. Nishino and the woman, the air surrounding the two of them, everything about it. At some point I must have begun sobbing. Much louder than the insects chirping in the clump of grass where I sat, I was now wailing the way I had when A-suke and B-maru died. Nishino was standing near me.

'Yamagata!' he said. Not with his grown-up voice, but with his year-nine voice.

'Yamagata, you should be ashamed,' Nishino said. I tried to stop, but I was still sniffling.

Nishino stood where he was, not saying anything more until I had composed myself.

'That was my sister,' he explained.

She was much older – a full twelve years – and just the other day her six-month-old baby had died, Nishino said softly.

It was her first child. Right after the funeral, his sister had taken to her bed. Her nerves were frayed. She couldn't be alone at home. She was wracked with anxiety unless someone was by her side at all times.

But even bed- and anxiety-ridden, she continued to produce milk – her breasts were full to bursting. Whenever she thought about the child she had lost, the milk would leak out. Going out soothed her anxiety somewhat. Seeing trees and grass and earth seemed to calm her.

'But once my sister had calmed down, she whispered to me, "I just want to die,"' Nishino told me. Astonished, I looked up at him. Nishino's expression was composed.

'But,' I stammered, and Nishino shook his head.

'That was my sister's way of trying to say, "It would be better that way." She can't find the words when there's so much sorrow. The same way that her breasts are tight and swollen with milk and she can barely stand the pain, all these thoughts in her head solidify in her body. It's agonizing. When the milk spurts out, the words burst from her lips – it's like something hardened has come loose, and she feels somewhat more at peace.'

'Nishino, are you . . . in love with your sister?' I asked gingerly.

'I feel sorry for her,' Nishino replied. He gazed off into the distance as he spoke.

I wanted to know what had happened to his sister's husband, but I couldn't bring myself to ask. The air between Nishino and his sister was not quite what might exist between lovers, although neither was it anything like that between family members.

'Yamagata, are you going out with Tanabe?' Nishino asked abruptly.

'Uh, yeah,' I answered. I may have had my doubts about whether or not Toru Tanabe and I were officially 'going out', but I nodded anyway.

'I see,' Nishino said. 'That's too bad, 'cause I kind of liked you too.'

'Huh?' The moment I looked into Nishino's eyes, he touched my chin with his fingers and, a thousand times more smoothly than Toru Tanabe, he tilted my head towards his and kissed me.

Nishino's lips parted and his saliva flowed into my mouth. It tasted sweet. Was this the taste of breast milk? Or was it the taste of Nishino? Without thinking, I put my arms around Nishino's waist, and held him tightly.

We kissed for a long time. Our kissing went on endlessly, with Nishino thinking of someone other than me, and me thinking of things other than Nishino.

In the grass, as I took in mouthfuls of Nishino, I remembered all of the things that I had buried in the vacant lot.

Kissing Nishino was wonderful. More wonderful than anything I had ever known. And kissing Nishino was also sad. It was one of the saddest moments I've ever known.

As I was kissing him, I thought to myself, *I may never come here again to bury something. I should tell my father that I don't need a birthday cake any more. Someday, I may be able to see my mother again. And from now on, I won't be afraid of growing up.*

Nishino's kiss accepted everything in my fourteen years,

and at the same time, his kiss rejected it in full. We kept kissing, fervently.

'Thank you, Nishino,' I said, once we had quite finished kissing.

'Uh-huh,' Nishino replied, and then said, 'Hey, why don't you get rid of Toru Tanabe, and go out with me?'

I glanced at Nishino with surprise, and saw a bashful look on his face as he stood up and gave the withering grass a swift kick.

'But, Nishino, you don't really like me that much, do you?' I asked.

'Yes, I do.'

'C'mon.' I peered into Nishino's face. Nishino turned just slightly away.

'A girl like you is too much for Toru Tanabe,' Nishino murmured.

'Is that so? But not too much for you, Nishino?' I asked.

'You're bold.'

'Tsk!' he responded.

Nishino came and sat back down next to me. We held hands for a little while. It was completely different from holding hands with Toru Tanabe. When I held Toru Tanabe's hand, it had felt like a strange creature from a faraway place. Big and warm, like something kind of scary I was seeing for the first time. But there was nothing the least bit odd about Nishino's hand. While we were holding hands, it felt as though I no longer knew where his hand stopped and mine began.

'I'm going to keep seeing Toru Tanabe,' I said.

'Humph,' Nishino snorted.

'Toru Tanabe is different from me, and that's why I'm going to keeping seeing him,' I repeated.

'Okay, okay, I got it,' Nishino replied, laughing. I laughed with him.

We both stood up at the same time. There were seeds from the grass stuck to the trousers of Nishino's school uniform, and to my skirt as well.


Autumn soon ended – before I knew it, winter arrived. The air was piercingly cold.

I conducted my tenth film appreciation with Toru Tanabe. After our ninth appreciation, we had coffee at the coffee shop and then, as we always did now, we went to the park, where I succeeded in kissing Toru Tanabe for the first time. Ever since that earlier attempt, Toru Tanabe had become very hesitant, and I couldn't help worrying about when we would actually succeed. After my kiss with Nishino, my feelings for Toru Tanabe had only grown stronger. In various ways.

Nishino and I still never spoke to each other in the classroom. I had stopped going to the vacant lot, so now I had practically no chance to talk to him.

When I happened to run into him on the way home one day, I asked Nishino about his sister.

'She's a little better.' Nishino answered the same way he did in class. With the bare minimum of words.

Time passed. I was thinking of chopping all my hair off. My mother had always worn her hair short. From her, I had inherited the same soft, fine hair, which tended to flatten against my small head. I thought that soon I might tell

Toru Tanabe about my mother. And then I might even tell him about my goldfish, Tara, and about the birthday cake with buttercream icing. I wondered what Toru Tanabe's face would look like while he listened to my stories.

Soon after winter began, the vacant lot was levelled and put up for sale. Sometimes, in the pale light of winter, I thought about Nishino. Once we had left middle school, I might not see him again but, through the various stages of life, I knew that I would remember Nishino often.

The small grass seeds stuck to Nishino's trousers. The many things buried in the vacant lot. The rock beside the magnolia tree. The feel of digging up the moist earth. And the mysterious, milk-sweet kiss.

I would always remember clearly what had happened in the grass between our fourteen-year-old selves, in the elusive space between adulthood and childhood.

# Goodnight

Yukihiko was savage.

Some people might be surprised to hear me call him that. They might think a word like 'savage' doesn't befit a man such as Yukihiko.

Thick hair. An angular but not too prominent chin. Deep, dark eyes. A mouth always turned up at the corners.

To this day, Yukihiko has never once raised his voice to me. Whenever he calls my name – Manami – his tone is soft. Yukihiko is always smiling. The moment he catches my eye, he looks as though he's about to burst into laughter. The smoothness under Yukihiko's chin. The shiver I feel when I touch the whiskers that are just starting to grow there.

Yukihiko left nothing to be desired, in any aspect.

This applied at the office as well. His subordinates trusted him. He was on friendly terms with his colleagues. His superiors liked to invite him out drinking. Yukihiko satisfied all of them, to an overly unobjectionable degree – it was actually quite boring.

Nevertheless, Yukihiko was savage.

Not because the first time Yukihiko kissed me was in the darkness, behind the closed doors of a conference room. And not because, right after his intense kiss, he pushed me down, bending me backwards over a desk, and slowly began to unbutton my blouse. Not even because, despite not knowing if anyone might catch us, he remained calm as he fastidiously caressed my bare skin. Nor was it because although I said, 'Stop,' over and over, each time he quietly replied, 'I will not stop.'

I never once acted as though I was in love with Yukihiko. I was Manami Enomoto, the deputy head of the division. Yukihiko Nishino was my subordinate. I was three years older than him. I had been at the company five years longer. We had never seen each other alone, nor had there ever been any hint of affection between us. Several times, the two of us went out to business meetings together – we took the train, and the bus if necessary, we had various appointments, then we took the train again (the bus too if necessary), and returned to the office. We would submit a meeting report and our expense slips, and be done with it – that was the extent of our work time together.

However, I was in love with Yukihiko, from the beginning. Every time I sensed Yukihiko pass behind my chair, the phrase 'mixing business with pleasure' flashed in my mind. I had always thought that I wanted to be successful at my job, and so I had no intention of conducting an affair at the office. Nevertheless, as soon as Yukihiko was assigned to my division, I fell in love with him.

Love? Even that word seems too tepid to describe what I

felt for him – 'besotted', or 'fervent' – less familiar words seem more apt. I was fervently, besottedly in love with Yukihiko. From the moment I met him.

And Yukihiko knew it. He knew, and didn't even bother to pretend otherwise. Despite his awareness that I didn't want him to know.

Yukihiko grasped perfectly that I was secretly in love with him, and that I was trying to quell these innermost feelings, by any means, yet he gave me no reprieve. There was no relief, no chance that I would be capable of extinguishing this passion on my own.

It was May when Yukihiko kissed me in the pitch-black conference room. It had been a year and a month since I first met him. In those thirteen months, I had become more infatuated, all the while trying to smother my ardour. Yukihiko's gaze, when directed at me, had always been remote. But the more I tried to suppress it, the more my passion grew.

That May, Yukihiko won me quite easily. Like a butterfly collector who spreads the wings of his specimen on a board, and pins them in place. Gently and carefully handling the now-dead body of an insect he has captured. I suppose you could say that Yukihiko had already entrapped me. Without us ever having shared a caress. Without us even having shared a glance.

If you had told me this before I met Yukihiko, I would have laughed in your face. 'What kind of nonsense are you talking about?' Love doesn't begin until you've got to know someone well enough. We're beyond the ridiculousness of youth. We're too old for falling in love with the idea of love. When you're a grown-up, love means being attracted to someone and wanting to be near them, reading and decoding the signs and scents the other gives off, communicating with each other, and sounding out how the other feels. That's what I would have told you, with a laugh. But you won't hear me laughing any more. Foolish love. Love that makes you go numb, that paralyzes you, that doubles you over like a wounded animal. Yukihiko used no weapons, he used no claws or talons or fangs, to deliver the injurious blow of his love – he won me quite easily. If you had seen the way that I trembled. The frissons that welled up within me. Frissons that erupted from the joy of being captured by Yukihiko.

The first time he touched me – gently but with confidence – Yukihiko was truly savage. Neither his bated breath, nor his tender caress, nor his soft voice could conceal Yukihiko's savagery. It's the nature of the beast, when capturing its prey. The brute seizes the smaller creature, with perfect grace and not a single wasted motion. The brute is all the more savage for his elegance and lack of frivolity.

'Manami . . .' Yukihiko had called my name. In the darkness of the conference room. In the shadows, with the shades lowered. I said nothing in reply. It came as a shock to me, that Yukihiko knew my first name, having only ever referred to me before as Ms Enomoto, Deputy Head of Division. It came as a shock to remember that I had this other name, to hear it melting sweetly on Yukihiko's lips for the first time. Behind my closed eyes, I saw the cloudless sky that must have been just outside the window. Yukihiko lay me down, my upper body resting on top of a desk in the conference room.

'No,' I said softly. I repeated the word over and over.

Yukihiko silenced me with his graceful savagery. Yukihiko made me utterly his own.

My body, my mind, my heart – these all belonged to me. And yet everything that was mine was also entirely Yukihiko's. From that day on, a year and a month after I had first met him. Even though a person can never really belong to someone else. Despite that, I wanted to become his. I had decided that I would give myself to him.

Of course, when the two of us emerged from the conference room, the corridor was deserted. Always careful Yukihiko. There was the slightest flush in my cheeks. Yukihiko's white shirt was spotless, and his necktie was perfectly knotted – he was cool and collected. I went left, and Yukihiko went right, as we parted. He went straight to the lift, pushed the button and stood there waiting. I opened the door to the emergency staircase, my heels clacking as I descended the steps. When I reached the floor below, I pressed my cheek against the steel door. The heavy door felt cool against my skin. I shed a few tears. Then I touched my hair to make sure that it wasn't out of place, softly wiped the tears from my chin with a handkerchief and blinked several times. I pushed open the steel door and dug my high heels into the beige wall-to-wall carpeting as I started walking.

Yukihiko was nowhere in sight on this floor. I exhaled softly as I passed behind the division manager, whose gaze was focused on a pile of documents. It seemed strange to me that I was still breathing. That I was standing up straight. The May sky was bright, and I was a strange being beneath it. I returned to my desk and popped a minty sweet into my mouth. And I quietly went back to work.

\*

Once, I met one of Yukihiko's old girlfriends.

'Kanoko,' Yukihiko called out to her. I was livid. Why would he call her name, in front of me? The name of a former girlfriend. And so tenderly too.

'Good evening. Nice to meet you.' These were the words that came out of my mouth, despite my fury.

'Kanoko has suggested that the three of us go out to eat together,' Yukihiko had told me a few days earlier.

'Who's this Kanoko?' I asked.

'A friend,' Yukihiko replied. He was caressing my buttocks at the time.

'Girls' bottoms are always so cool, so smooth – I love them . . .' Yukihiko murmured contentedly.

'Your bottom is cool too. Why don't you play with your own?' I replied. Yukihiko chuckled. I did too. But while I was laughing, I was also imagining what this 'Kanoko' was like.

'Manami, what is it that you like about Yukihiko?' Kanoko asked me. What a bitch. I became livid, but my outward expression did not betray my fury. I merely smiled timidly.

Yukihiko remained calm throughout the meal. Everything was extremely proper. We drank an appropriate amount of saké. The conversation was innocuous. The evening wore on, gradually. Kanoko seemed to have decided to treat me lightly. *Oh, this woman is Yukihiko's new girlfriend? How boring!* She barely even tried to conceal these thoughts. For my part, I behaved like an adult (like a sensible, mature woman three years their senior), drinking my saké with a radiant smile and when the dessert of pear sorbet arrived, dipping my gleaming silver spoon into it with relish.

When at last we parted from Kanoko, I promptly turned my back to Yukihiko and started walking briskly.

'What's the matter, Manami?' Yukihiko asked, chasing after me. I didn't answer, I just kept walking. As forcefully as a mammoth striding across the tundra.

'Are you angry?' Brisk, brisk. 'I don't get it.' Brisk, brisk.

Eventually Yukihiko came around in front of me and embraced me tightly. I exploded. Like I really meant it. Yukihiko immediately withdrew from me.

'Why would you introduce me to one of your old girlfriends?' I thundered. Yukihiko's mouth was slightly agape.

'You could tell?'

'It was completely obvious!'

'But, how'd you know?'

'I'd have to be stupid not to!'

'You think so?'

'You're so insensitive!'

'Me, insensitive?'

'You lack any delicacy!'

'I have no delicacy?'

'You're a man-child!'

'Me, a man-child?'

Yukihiko repeated everything after me, with a genuinely awestruck expression. I rapidly lost steam, crouching down where I was and starting to sob. After letting me cry for a moment, Yukihiko crooked his arms under my armpits and brought me swiftly upright. Then he lifted my chin and kissed me. Twice, three times – Yukihiko's light kisses were like a ripple. I leaned against him and continued to sob.

'I'm sorry,' Yukihiko said. I nodded, through my tears.

Yukihiko apologized again. I clung tightly to him. I was aware of how preciously I was behaving, yet still I clung to Yukihiko. I hated precious women. I didn't want to be one. At that moment, in the midst of my preciousness, I resolved never to call Yukihiko again. Having turned into something I despised, I had to impose at least certain strictures on myself. And so I vowed this to myself.


The moment when Yukihiko fell in love with me . . .

Even once the two of us started seeing each other, even once I started staying over at Yukihiko's apartment (for the same reason I wouldn't call him on the phone, I refused to let him into my apartment), Yukihiko didn't have strong feelings for me. Somehow I just knew this. Yukihiko maintained a smooth abstraction. That smoothness made it impossible to tell, without paying very close attention, whether he really was lost in his own world or not.

It was the mechanical clock.

What part of Tokyo was it? We had probably gone to see a movie. It was spring, and I had taken off my long-sleeved jacket and was carrying it over one arm. From the window of the train, I remember seeing many of the embankments in bloom with yellow rapeseed blossoms and pale violet cress. Yukihiko and I walked side by side on the street to the cinema. The asphalt had vibrated under our feet.

It was noon. The people walking ahead of us suddenly

stopped and looked up at the sky. A couple diagonally to the side of us looked upwards at the same angle. Yukihiko and I stopped walking too. There were clouds floating in the sky, but nothing else.

'There isn't anything to see,' I said, just as Yukihiko pointed in the general direction of the roof of the department store across from us.

'There!' he said.

Yukihiko was pointing at a marionette clock. A number of figures were emerging and then disappearing, as a cheerful yet melancholy tune played. There were bells clanging. The passers-by – all of them – had stopped and were looking up at it.

'If I could, I would like to be one of those frog dolls,' I said.

Yukihiko and I stood still, holding hands, even after the clock had finished chiming and the people looking up at it had started walking again. The frog doll had appeared from behind the four on the clock's dial. After emerging, it had frozen for a moment before spinning around once. Almost as if it were doing a somersault. And then it quickly retreated.

'Why the frog, when there are others like the prince and princess?' Yukihiko asked.

'I just think it's the frog for me, for whatever reason.'

'Hmm.'

Yukihiko left it at that. Then we saw a film (it was filled with action and tears and had a happy ending – those were Yukihiko's favourites), drank some tea, wandered around and, when evening came, we ate some curry (Yukihiko said that he could eat curry morning, noon and night, for days on end) and drank some beer. But the whole time, Yukihiko seemed preoccupied by something.

'That question before, I asked it wrong,' Yukihiko said, all of a sudden. He had finished his curry, and had just ordered some spicy chicken, a salad with hard-boiled egg and more beer.

'Instead of "why the frog?" I should have asked, "why a mechanical doll?" Whether it's the frog or the princess or the prince – it doesn't really matter.'

I stammered a non-reply. I had already forgotten why I had said that I wanted to be the frog on the marionette clock. But Yukihiko was looking at me so earnestly, I desperately tried to remember.

'Uh, well, a mechanical doll spends most of the time standing there in the dark, right?' I began tentatively.

'Uh-huh.' Yukihiko nodded gravely.

'And then, they come out once an hour, right?'

'Uh-huh.'

'Let's see ... when they come out, they dance and sing merrily, you know?'

'Uh-huh.'

'And then they go back to the dark, right?'

'Uh-huh.'

'They repeat this, forever and ever – until they break down.'

Yukihiko nodded again in reply, but with a slight frown. He picked up a piece of the spicy chicken, which had arrived, and bit into it.

'That's all.'

'Uh-huh,' Yukihiko said. He gnawed on the chicken,

without saying anything else. Then he ate almost all of the egg out of the salad (when it came to eggs, whether they were hard-boiled, scrambled, fried, in an omelette, sunny-side up, or raw – Yukihiko liked them all). He drained the last of his beer. His cheeks flushed and he frowned again as he said, 'I'm done for.'

Yukihiko was now in love with me.

I knew at that moment. With absolute clarity.

'You're done for what?' I asked, but Yukihiko didn't answer me. What could he have said? Up until that point, Yukihiko had never really been in love with a girl. Yukihiko the fearful.

Despite how graciously he treated women. Despite how savage he could be. Yukihiko was always afraid.

Of what?

Perhaps of everything related to the words 'forever' and 'ever'. Perhaps of the faint scent that a person gave off in the warmth of her breath. Perhaps even of the fragrant dew that came from the sky or the ground or running water.

For Yukihiko, these kinds of things were to be feared, as were the women associated with them, and he certainly hadn't fallen in love with any of them. It wasn't that he tried so hard not to fall in love – rather it was perfectly natural for him not to feel love. He wasn't capable of it.

But now, he was in love with me.

'Shall we go?' Yukihiko said quietly. Two pieces of spicy chicken remained on the plate, and the red leaf lettuce, mushrooms, rocket and walnuts were still in the salad, but Yukihiko left it all as he quickly stood up. He paid at the till, took me to the nearest station and then walked off. Into the night. Into the dark streets. Into the hard, unforgiving air (air so brittle that Yukihiko would need to be as serene as ever to maintain his calm).

How long would Yukihiko's inclination towards me last?

'I hate it when you're not around, Manami,' Yukihiko said. He seemed not at all happy. Genuinely troubled.

'I'll always be by your side,' I replied.

'That's not possible.'

'Well, if you're splitting hairs . . .'

'Manami, you'll never age?'

'I'm sure I will.'

'Manami, you won't gain or lose weight?'

'No doubt I'll get fat. Over the next ten years.'

'Manami, you'll always accept me as I am?'

'I'm not the Virgin Mary, am I?'

'Manami, will you always have sex with me?'

'Depending on the time and the place.'

'When you say "time and place", you mean that it won't always be OK?'

'Because there are various times and places.'

'Manami, will you get sick of me?'

'Come, now.'

'Maybe I'll get sick of you?'

'Shut up,' I said, flinging a cushion at Yukihiko. Sometimes I pushed him down. Or got up to make tea.

The truth was, Yukihiko had become terribly annoying. Some of the time. While he inclined himself towards me.

'I wonder if I'm in love with you?' Yukihiko would ask me.

'Figure it out yourself.'

'I get scared when I think about it on my own.'

There had always been something awkward about Yukihiko. Despite how slick his actions, his words, his movements were. Despite how smooth and flawless he could be. There was something about Yukihiko, something about his being that had been awkward.

'I've been awkward since birth,' Yukihiko sighed.

'Since birth?'

'Yes, since birth. Part of my brain, or some other part of me – my kidneys or my liver – must be artificial.'

'Is that true?' I asked, and Yukihiko nodded deeply.

'My mother and father and my older sister – they surrounded me with love. It was too much – they spoiled me. It must have been because I'm an artificial human, and they felt sorry for me.' Yukihiko said this very earnestly.

'But what's so bad about being artificial,' I murmured as I stroked Yukihiko's cheek.

He shook his head. 'It's no good.'

'It's fine – I still love you, even if you're artificial.'

'Nope, it's no good.'

'Why not?'

'Because, if I'm artificial, one day I'll stop loving you.'

'Is that so?'

'Yes. It's a known fact that artificial humans cannot mix with real humans.'

'You don't have to say such things.' I think that's what I told him. 'Even if you were to stop loving me, I would still love you, Yukihiko.'

Yukihiko wore a forlorn expression. 'To make a woman

say something like that, I must be a total jerk,' he said, and took me in his arms. *You really are a jerk*, I thought to myself. *And I'm just as much of a jerk*, I also told myself.

We held each other. Gently. Like water. But without actually turning into water.

We were anxious. We were light. We had been rapturously happy. We had been in despair. We had been on the verge of loving one another. But, incapable of doing so, we found ourselves on the precipice, doomed to remain there forever.


And so, Yukihiko got sick of me.

It pains me to use those words, but they're the ones that best fit.

Yukihiko got sick of me.

When Yukihiko said to me, 'I love bean-paste doughnuts,' that's when I knew.

'I don't care much for them,' I replied.

Yukihiko had been leaning against the headboard, reading a magazine. I had been sitting on the carpet, half-watching a late-night movie. It was a sad movie, in black and white. Not the kind of movie that Yukihiko cared much for. There wasn't enough action or dancing. That's what he would have said about this movie.

At some point, Yukihiko had regained his smoothness. That same smooth abstraction. He had at last got sick of me.

'What about melon pan?'

'For some reason, melon pan makes me sad.' I had been blowing my nose as I said this. I had shed a tear or two. The realization that Yukihiko was no longer inclined towards me had thrown me into a panic. But maybe it wasn't too late yet. There was no need for tears. Maybe it wasn't too late. Too late? For what?

'Manami.' Yukihiko said my name. In a calm voice.

I did not want to hear whatever words would follow. Manami, let's break up. Manami, it turns out this Sunday is no good for me. Manami, I'm not interested in you any more. I wanted to cover my ears. But instead I slowly turned in Yukihiko's direction, and just smiled at him.

'What is it?'

'There's nothing sad about curry buns, is there?'

'No, there isn't,' I replied. I had to laugh (at Yukihiko's beloved curry, stuffed in bread. At my beloved Yukihiko. At the Yukihiko who no longer loved me).

Yukihiko did not yet know that he was sick of me. I wondered if I should tell him. But there was still a faint glimmer of hope – what if I was wrong?

'Why are you crying?' Yukihiko asked. At some point I had started openly weeping. Heedlessly.

'The movie, it's so sad.'

'I don't know why you bother watching such sad movies,' Yukihiko muttered, and went back to his magazine.

I blew my nose again. After that, I didn't shed another tear. I turned and saw that Yukihiko had fallen asleep. With the magazine still open on his chest.

'Wake up, Yukihiko! You haven't taken your night-time vitamin B1 and C,' (Yukihiko believed that it was more effective to take individual supplements rather than a multivitamin), 'and your gingko biloba extract.' I shook him awake as I said this.

'Hmm, what happened?' Yukihiko murmured. I touched his arm. It felt much more muscular than it looked.

*Poor Yukihiko*, I thought, as I stroked his arm. For whatever reason, I did not think, *Poor me*. Just, *Poor Yukihiko*. Soon Yukihiko might break up with me. Soon Yukihiko might be the one to leave me. I couldn't help but feel sorry for how Yukihiko would be, after he broke up with me, after he left me. I was simply awash with pity for him.

No matter how I tried, I couldn't wake up Yukihiko, so on my own I took gingko biloba extract and a multivitamin (I believed multivitamins were just as effective). I turned out the lights, and slid into bed beside Yukihiko. I kissed him on the forehead, and closed my eyes.


'Why do people have to change?' Yukihiko asked.

It was raining outside. Perfect weather for this.

*Here it comes . . .* I sighed. And then, a strange fighting spirit welled up in me. I didn't know if it was a fighting spirit, or a sense of accomplishment?

'It's human nature to change,' I said, and Yukihiko snorted.

'Manami, that's such a logical thing to say.'

'Well, after all, I am a logical, single, thirty-three-year-old woman who's your superior!'

Then I realized it was going on three years since I had first met Yukihiko. I was taken by surprise. I wasn't sure whether three years was a long time, or no time at all.

Yukihiko was looking out at the rain. It was falling in huge drops. The huge raindrops of early spring.

'I love you, Manami,' Yukihiko said.

'But, you want to break up, don't you?'

Yukihiko looked at me sharply. His cheeks were taut with nervousness. It seemed as though he hadn't been expecting to hear that.

'You're breaking up with me, aren't you?' I repeated it.

'Manami.' Yukihiko was clearly surprised. I was even more surprised to see him surprised.

'Why are you so shocked?' I asked.

'Because I've just told you that I love you.'

'But, Yukihiko, you're not interested in me any more.'

'That's not true.'

'But it is true.'

Yukihiko had turned pale. He had underestimated me. All along. Even though I had not underestimated him. But, how do you love someone without blinding yourself? Don't we all have to indulge each other, let our guard down and – ever so slightly – lower ourselves, in order to love someone else? Yet I had never allowed myself to underestimate Yukihiko – not for a single moment.

'Manami.' Yukihiko called my name. In a plaintive voice. 'Why are you saying these things, Manami?'

But Yukihiko had already realized it. That I was aware of his smooth indifference. There was no going back. Now it really was too late. I had led Yukihiko to the point where there was no longer a glimmer of hope.

The rain grew heavier. It really was the perfect weather.

I left Yukihiko's apartment alone. I closed the door quietly behind me. Yukihiko had followed me to the door. Like a faithful dog. There wasn't a shred of the savagery of that first time. Just as if I had been the one to break up with him.

'Goodbye,' I said, but Yukihiko wouldn't say goodbye.

'Why?' he said. This time I was the one who remained silent. And then I went out into the rain.

Even while I was walking through the rain, a strange feeling – which felt like a sense of accomplishment – remained in my body. The rain swept in at a sharp angle under my umbrella.

I told myself I was okay with not belonging to Yukihiko any more, and I kept walking, taking long strides.


There's more to the story of Yukihiko and me.

For a while, Yukihiko called me every day. Needless to say, I never called him. (My resolution, from before. I kept it, fiercely. To the end.)

'How did you know, Manami, that I didn't love you any more?' Yukihiko always asked. And every time, my reply was, 'Yukihiko, you never loved me in the first place, did you?'

'But, Manami, I could say the same about you,' Yukihiko said.

'Perhaps,' I replied, but it wasn't true. Yukihiko had given me no choice. Yukihiko, so stubborn about being loveless. And me, always second-guessing him. We were a poor match.

After that, for a while, I took great care to make sure that the two of us were never alone together.

A few months later, Yukihiko was transferred to a different floor. Soon after, he became assistant head of his department (a position just slightly above deputy head – my title).

'Let's celebrate!' he said when he invited me out that evening. *By now, it should be all right*, I thought to myself. By now, things had simmered down.

'Why can't I love a woman?' Yukihiko said, resting his elbows on the counter.

We were sitting on stools in a small bar.

'I wonder why,' I replied softly, sipping a gin and tonic.

'Is there something wrong with me?'

'Isn't it a good sign, that you can recognize there might be something wrong with you?'

'You're so mean, Manami.'

Yukihiko exhaled cigarette smoke. Apparently he had started smoking after we broke up.

'The sushi was tasty,' he said.

'And kind of expensive,' I replied.

'I'll get this,' he offered.

Yukihiko put out his cigarette. In the short time since we had broken up, Yukihiko seemed a bit more mature. I realized in that instant that I still loved him. I was filled with intense regret, wondering why I had let Yukihiko go. And yet, I knew that it was wrong to think about it in terms of letting him go or being the one to end things. It was simply over. Everything was.

So when Yukihiko invited me to his apartment that night, I nodded without hesitation. Not because I was happy. Quite the contrary. Because I wasn't particularly happy at all.

*It'll be all right*, I reassured myself. It would be madness to want to belong to Yukihiko again. *Don't even think it, okay?*

*Okay*, I replied to the version of myself in my head. I'd

known as much sadness as I could bear. I had dwelled on it long enough.

Yukihiko took my hand with his usual smoothness.

'You smell good,' he murmured as he brought his face to my chest. Yukihiko's apartment was almost unchanged. As if it were perfectly natural, I let him undress me (Yukihiko had always hated for me to take my own clothes off), and then, following a precise routine, we had sex. I thoroughly enjoyed myself. And I think Yukihiko did too.

Afterwards, when I went to put on my underwear, Yukihiko grabbed my arm.

'Stay over!'

'I've got an early start tomorrow.'

'Hey . . . marry me!'

'You fool. Don't joke about it,' I said, as I fastened the hook on my bra. I was already running through tomorrow's list of things to do in my head. I heard a strange sound. Like the noise of a radio that wasn't tuned to a station.

Yukihiko was moaning.

'Why am I so messed up?' he said through his groans. I had never seen his face look like this before. Yukihiko's expression was different from the graceful savagery of the early days, different from the anxiety-ridden days of when he used to incline himself towards me.

'Messed up?' I repeated slowly, as I buttoned my blouse.

'I wanted to stay in love with you always!'

I finished buttoning up my blouse and started putting on my stockings.

'I planned to be with you for the rest of my life!'

'You don't have to say that.' Quietly, I fastened my skirt.

'Why can't I love someone properly?'

It's just not in your nature, I was about to say, but I stopped myself. Because I felt sorry for Yukihiko now. It was just like that time when I had watched his face, while he was sleeping. Poor Yukihiko. Whether it was his own fault, I wasn't sure.

'Someday there'll be someone you can love,' I said tenderly, slipping on my blazer. *Even though you don't really want someone to love,* I was thinking.

'Manami.' Yukihiko called my name in a low voice.

'What is it,' I replied. I looked at my wristwatch with an exaggerated gesture.

'Manami, goodnight.' Yukihiko hung his head.

'Goodnight, Yukihiko,' I said in response, turning to face him properly.

I shut the door to Yukihiko's apartment. The grassy scent of the June air hit my nose.

'Poor Yukihiko,' I murmured. *Poor me,* I thought, but I stopped myself. Because there was no longer anything the slightest bit pitiful about me. Instead, I prayed for Yukihiko's happiness.

I was not in the habit of praying for anyone's happiness, so I didn't know how to go about it, but when I was a child I had read in a storybook about one way to do it, so I followed that.

First, I put my left hand in my right pocket and said, 'May Yukihiko be happy.' Then, I put my right hand in my left pocket and said once again, 'May Yukihiko be happy.' I performed the ritual very carefully, and once I had completed it, I turned in the direction of Yukihiko's apartment.

'Goodnight, poor Yukihiko,' I whispered. June's cool night-time air gently enveloped me.

I thought I could hear Yukihiko's voice say, *Goodnight, Manami*, but I knew it was just in my head. Slowly, I started walking.

# The Heart Races

Wearing a yukata was nice and everything – the crisp cotton was perfect for summer's heat – but it loosened up just from walking around. I thought I had put it on properly, but still it came undone at the front. This always happened to me. 'Dope,' Yukihiko said.

'Don't call me a dope!' I exclaimed. But no matter how I pleaded, Yukihiko wouldn't stop. I didn't know what to do with my yukata that just got looser and looser, so Yukihiko stood behind me, encircling my torso with his arms. He untied my obi sash.

'Hold still. Cross it over properly in front,' Yukihiko said. I stood there idly as he adjusted the crossing of each side of the yukata. He took the untied obi in his hands and stretched it out with a snap.

'Your obi was twisted.'

'Really?' I asked.

'You're the one who tied it?'

'I thought I'd tied it neatly.'

'There was nothing neat about it. You're hopeless,' Yukihiko said, his arms surrounding my torso again as he tied the obi for me. He pulled the knot tight, the fabric of the sash making a pleasant squeaking sound.

'Thank you, Mr Wardrobe Assistant,' I said, imitating a Kyoto accent, and Yukihiko frowned. He may have been standing behind me, so I couldn't see him frown, but there was no question that there was a frown on his face.

'I'm not your assistant!'

'Yukihiko, you're good at everything,' I said. Yukihiko came around in front of me. And indeed, he was frowning. Although his expression was soft. The sweetness in his face, his tidiness, the precision with which he had tied my obi for me – these were Yukihiko's distinguishing characteristics.

Women liked Yukihiko. When I called him on the phone late at night, he took forever to answer. The phone would ring and ring, but if I was patient, he'd finally pick up on the twelfth ring with a low and deep, 'Yes?' At night, Yukihiko was always fielding calls from one girl or another.

'I have another call,' he'd say to the girl on the phone. 'Gotta go. Good to talk to you,' Yukihiko would sign off. This may have accounted for why it took so many rings for him to answer. When he finally switched over to my call on the twelfth ring, he'd automatically reply, 'Yes?' I bet he used the same voice with every girl. It was an all-purpose monotone. A voice he could use in any situation – when having a fight with a girl, when making a move on her, or even when he was breaking up with her.

Once he knew it was me calling, Yukihiko's voice got a little deeper. 'Ah, is that you, Kanoko?' he'd say with a sigh. And then his voice would revert back to the smooth monotone reserved for girls. 'What's going on with you today?' he'd ask.

I'd murmur my assent. 'Not much really going on with me. What about you, Yukihiko? How've you been?'

'Oh, you know, I'm fine,' Yukihiko would reply. Sometimes I could hear the sound of a call waiting, but Yukihiko never clicked over while he was on the phone with me. No matter how frivolous the conversation was or how endlessly it went on, he never clicked over.

'Manami doesn't get angry?' I tried asking Yukihiko, just once. Manami was Yukihiko's girlfriend. A beautiful woman three years older than him.

'If she calls and it doesn't go to voicemail, and you don't pick up on call waiting, won't she know that you're talking to someone?' I asked.

Yukihiko laughed. 'I'm the one who calls Manami.'

'She doesn't call you?'

'Nope.'

'Hmm,' I murmured, and quickly changed the subject. I was always the one who called Yukihiko. He almost never called me. Even when Yukihiko and I had been boyfriend and girlfriend, I had always called him. Yukihiko had always been the one waiting.

Yukihiko and I had broken up five years ago, shortly after I graduated from university. I was the one who suggested we break up. When I told him I had met someone else, Yukihiko just hung his head for a moment before looking up at me and saying, 'Well then, I guess there's nothing I can do.'

I had expected him to put up more of a fight, and then I felt as though I had been sidestepped. Not that it was a big deal, since I had been the one to suggest it in the first place, but, yeah – I'd been dodged.

Even now, whenever Yukihiko and I are together, people usually ask if we are boyfriend and girlfriend. One time when an acquaintance asked me, I denied it categorically, though with an odd look on my face. Even I knew that my denial had been just a tad too outright. On the other hand, when people asked Yukihiko the same thing, he would reply, 'Don't I wish.' With a smile. Implying plenty of assurance.

My obi now tightly knotted, I stood behind Yukihiko and watched as he locked the door to our room. Yukihiko looked dashing in his yukata. On me, the yukata provided by the ryokan where we were staying immediately sagged and drooped, but somehow Yukihiko always managed to keep his looking crisp, as if it were still brand new.

Yukihiko turned to me as I stood idly in the hallway. 'You there! What are you waiting for?' he called out. Caught off guard, I looked up in surprise. Yukihiko's face wore a combination of scowl and smile.

'You've made no progress at all!' Yukihiko chided, taking my hand.

'That's not true,' I replied, and Yukihiko laughed mockingly, but his voice was sweet.

'Hurry up, then!' Yukihiko said, letting go of my hand. It had been so long since Yukihiko had held my hand – this was the first time since we had broken up five years ago. I had been certain that being touched by Yukihiko would send me into a fluster, but that didn't happen.

Yukihiko and I had come to stay at this ryokan for a night. The truth was that I had planned to be here with my boyfriend. Something had come up at the last minute and he wasn't able to come. I had asked my girlfriends, but they were all busy – either they were married, or spending time with their own boyfriends, or studying for a qualifying exam. As a last resort – and half in jest – I mentioned the idea to Yukihiko.

'Sure, I'll go,' Yukihiko had replied, as if it were no big deal.

'What about Manami?' I asked, and Yukihiko laughed.

'Manami is busy. She works weekends too,' he said. Manami was Yukihiko's boss. Three years older, beautiful, she was not only his boss, but his lover. Yukihiko referred to her as 'top-notch'.

I strained my ear to tell whether or not Yukihiko's laugh betrayed a tinge of loneliness at not being able to spend weekends with Manami, but I couldn't be sure over the phone. His voice had the same soft all-purpose monotone as always.

The meal was great. The menu at this ryokan had been created to complement Japanese saké. I like saké, so it follows that I enjoy cuisine that pairs well with it. There were large plates of sashimi, daringly heaped with Japanese sea bass and bonito. There were also raw whelks and *kohada* gizzard shad, tightened with salt and vinegar. All accompanied with plenty of delicate and aromatic *iwanori* seaweed.

'This is *modorigatsuo*, the bonito that has returned for the autumn,' I said, and Yukihiko nodded indifferently.

'The meals at these kinds of inns are good, but they're pretty standard,' he said in reply.

'There's nothing standard about it – there are subtle distinctions.'

'Um-hmm.'

With this murmured response, Yukihiko reached for a piece of rolled omelette with his chopsticks. Yukihiko barely drank at all. He could opine about ice cream, or ganache, or bean-jam buns, but if you tried to have a conversation with him about the refreshing first sip of beer, you would get nowhere. My boyfriend was a drinker. We had chosen this ryokan specifically because we'd heard the food was good. It made me wonder what kind of places Yukihiko and Manami went to when they travelled together.

Manami was the type of woman who could drink in moderation, but who also enjoyed dessert. I had dinner with the two of them after they became an item. How had I got myself into such a situation? I was not such an idiot as to have brazenly inserted myself into an old boyfriend's date with his new girlfriend – that had not been my intention – but somehow it was how things ended up.

Manami was polite from start to finish – her cheerfulness was resolute. She didn't clutch Yukihiko's hand under the table, nor did she ever whisper to him any prompts about leaving – not even when I thanked them at the end of the evening. We all behaved perfectly amicably, extending our meal over three different venues.

'I don't know how you can imbibe so much fluid,' Yukihiko had commented to me, after settling his stomach with a ginger ale.

'As long as it's saké, there's no limit. Right?' I responded. I had been seeking assent from Manami, but she merely nodded in a modest and ambiguous manner. The gesture of her head was utterly restrained – refuting neither Yukihiko's opinion nor my own. As I gazed into Manami's eyes, moist like those of a herbivorous animal, I somehow felt quite sorry for her.

'What is it you like about Yukihiko?' I asked Manami. I was definitely being bitchy. I felt terribly contemptuous, but whether it was directed towards Manami, or towards Yukihiko, or towards the world in general, I wasn't sure. When I start to pity someone, my contempt knows no bounds.

'Well . . .' Manami tilted her head.

'Cut it out – don't pick a fight,' Yukihiko said from the sidelines, but I paid him no heed.

'I mean, I'm sure that when it comes to men, Manami, you have much better options,' I went on.

With a grave expression, Manami considered this for a moment, and then she replied, 'I don't think of it in terms of Yukihiko's faults or assets.'

I may have emitted a sound of surprise.

'I think I would love Yukihiko no matter what kind of person he was.'

Manami smiled a beautiful smile. I was clobbered. How was it that a person like her existed? An attitude at the perfect temperature. Meticulously chosen words. And always, her demeanour remained unruffled.

I decided that I would hate Manami, from that moment on. But I couldn't. Manami was too reasonable in the face of hatred. And pride wouldn't allow me to hate Yukihiko's girlfriend. *Pride in what?* I scoffed.

*

After we had finished our meal, Yukihiko and I went out to the beach. We donned haori jackets over our yukata. In this town on the Pacific Ocean, the temperature was the slightest bit warmer than in Tokyo. Still, the evening breeze was cool as it caressed our cheeks. We could see fires for luring fish at night, burning on the boats offshore.

'They must be fishing for squid.'

'Probably,' Yukihiko replied nonchalantly.

Since he and I had broken up, Yukihiko seemed to have become more and more attractive to women. 'You're so popular,' I had teased him, but Yukihiko always shook his head.

'It's not that I'm popular, it's that they're lonely,' he replied. You fool, I wanted to shout at him. You sound like the leader of a religious cult. But I couldn't bring myself to yell at Yukihiko. Because, no matter what, I'd always be the one to call him up on the phone. Even when I had a boyfriend, or despite the fact that work was going fine, or if I had plenty of friends to talk to – the night would wear on and I'd end up calling Yukihiko.

'Aren't there squid that are luminescent?' Yukihiko said.

'You mean firefly squid?'

'Right, right – fireflies.'

'Not fireflies – firefly squid.'

'One time, someone made me eat one of those fireflies while it was still alive.'

The air was moving in my direction from behind Yukihiko. The scent of soap wafted from Yukihiko's body.

'Sounds delicious.'

'You eat it right away, one that's just been swimming right before your eyes.'

'But wasn't it delicious?'

'It was good. But I can't do that kind of thing,' Yukihiko said.

'What do you mean, "that kind of thing"?' I asked.

'That kind of thing,' Yukihiko repeated.

'Wait a minute, Yukihiko – are you sentimental?' I asked.

'Yeah, I guess so,' Yukihiko replied, in a deep and soft voice. The scent of soap radiated from him again.

I was suddenly seized by an urge to touch him. Yukihiko's supple fingers. His warm palms. There on the seashore at night, I gently reached out my hand towards Yukihiko. Just as I was about to touch him, he spoke again.

'You've always been that way, Kanoko. Calm and casual about sheer brutality.'

The tide came in quietly. Yukihiko and I were sitting on a piece of driftwood.

I could feel the warmth of the driftwood through the thin cotton of my yukata. The heat was left over from the day's sunshine.

A tiny crab scurried over my foot, clad in the inn's sandals which I had slipped on.

The beach was illuminated by the roadway lighting. Every so often a heavy truck passed by on the main road that ran along the shoreline. The dim light that surrounded us where we were sitting did not reach as far as the water's edge.

We could only sense the waves advancing and retreating in the darkness.

I gazed at Yukihiko's profile in the gauzy light. His skin was rougher now, compared to when he was in his twenties. His cheekbones were pronounced. His beard had got thicker too. I was thinking about what he had said to me earlier. Was I really brutal? Had I always been?

I couldn't remember much of the details from when Yukihiko and I were boyfriend and girlfriend. I had hardly been thinking about anything, back then. Yukihiko had loved me, he had wanted to sleep with me, he had wanted to make me happy – I had taken each of these things as a given. It had never even occurred to me that they bordered on miraculous.

I loved Yukihiko. I loved my father. I loved my mother. I loved my cat, Kuro. I loved the newborn baby from the house next door. I loved the smell of sunshine on clean laundry. I loved skipping school on rainy days. I loved Yukihiko in the same way I loved these things. Yet I wasn't able to remember why I had gone and fallen in love with someone who wasn't him.

'Kanoko, you're like a bird in the sky,' Yukihiko had once said to me, about three months after we had broken up.

Ever since right after we ended things, we had maintained the same close friendship that we had now.

'What do you mean by that?' I had asked him.

'Birds, you know, they're dependent upon the wind, right? When the southern breeze begins to blow, they ride the wind to fly north, and when the northern wind blows, they return to the south. Whenever the wind changes, they forget all about everything that happened up until yesterday, and happily fly off, twittering all the way.' Yukihiko chuckled as he gave this explanation.

'I am not a bird,' I had replied indignantly. But while Yukihiko had been talking, I had found myself feeling more and more like his foolish little bird that happily thinks of nothing at all.

'See? That's you, Kanoko. You were like that when we were together, and you're still like that now.' Yukihiko had been staring at my fringe as he spoke.

I've always hated my forehead, so back then I used to have a fringe. When we had been boyfriend and girlfriend, Yukihiko would constantly try to sweep it back. Then he thought it was amusing to criticize my exposed forehead. I'd squirm to avoid his efforts to push my hair aside, but often found myself lying under Yukihiko, and we'd end up having sex.

Yukihiko's fingers were about to touch my fringe. In those three months since we had broken up, his fingers hadn't touched me at all. I drew my face towards Yukihiko. It was an involuntary movement. Yukihiko's fingers seemed to gravitate towards my forehead. I uttered a little sound, and when I did, Yukihiko made a similar noise himself. He immediately withdrew his hand. The two of us were silent for a moment, and then we burst into laughter at the same time. Yukihiko's laugh was easy-going, while mine was a bit stiff.

'Birds have troubles too – you'd be surprised,' I said through my stiffened laughter. Yukihiko nodded.

'Everyone always expects Kanoko the bird to chirp away

cheerfully all the time,' he said. There was such serenity in what Yukihiko said that I found it a bit annoying. After all, I had been the one who said we should break up. I should be the one who felt serene. However, after we broke up, I was forever the one who was stiff, while Yukihiko was always perfectly relaxed and easy-going.

Soon after that, I stopped seeing the guy that I'd ended things with Yukihiko for. In my memory, that dalliance lasted less than six months. Needless to say, Yukihiko and I did not revive our relationship. We may not have got back together, but we remained close friends. Sometimes we'd meet up for tea. And we talked on the phone constantly. Even though we had broken up, things were good. That was how it was with Yukihiko and me. I was quite pleased about that. Or I should have been.

'Yukihiko, why did you come here with me?' I asked. The tide was coming in. The entire ocean had expanded in the night, and it felt as if the air had become much more condensed and heavy.

'Why did I . . . ?' Yukihiko replied leisurely.

I rested my head against Yukihiko's shoulder. His arm remained where it was, without embracing me. I was the one who put my arm around Yukihiko's waist and held him.

'It's hot,' Yukihiko said.

'You'll be fine.'

'Kanoko, are you happy now?' Yukihiko asked suddenly. Are you lonely or are you happy? – just like the leader of a religious cult.

'Hey, let's go back to the inn and have sex,' I said, ignoring Yukihiko's question.

'Let's not,' Yukihiko replied, letting his arm remain limp.

'Then, why did you come here, Yukihiko?'

'Kanoko, maybe you're a nymphomaniac?'

'Drop dead, Yukihiko.'

My eyes had adjusted to the darkness, and I could now faintly make out the ocean moving in the night. The surface of the water was smooth. That smoothness was inching up the shore.

Yukihiko put his arm around my shoulder. He held me softly at first, then gradually with more strength. I remembered what Yukihiko's body had felt like when we were lovers, and the way he used to make love to me. I remembered the way that I had loved Yukihiko. I remembered it very clearly. But in the midst of remembering, I also realized that, here, in the present moment, I had never completely lost the sensation of these things.

'Yukihiko,' I said softly. How many years had it been since I had called his name like that.

'Kanoko,' Yukihiko said, his voice deep.

We stayed like that for a long time, holding each other's shoulder and waist tightly. The waves had come almost all the way up to our feet.

Yukihiko's lips grazed my cheek. I planted a light kiss on his neck.

'The night seems immense, doesn't it?'

'It does.'

'Yukihiko, you know I love you.'

'Me too. I'll always love you, Kanoko.'

'That's not what I mean.'

'It's no use,' Yukihiko said without hesitation, still holding my shoulder tightly.

'Huh?'

'It's over between us.'

I made another idiotic sound.

'It's over, don't you know that?' Yukihiko said, with warmth in his voice.

'Is it really over?' I repeated, like an idiot.

'It is,' Yukihiko reiterated.

I felt as if my mind had gone completely blank.

It was true, I thought. Yukihiko and I, we weren't far apart, but we were each in our respective places, separate from one another.

And although I was here now, and Yukihiko was here too, that was all it meant.

That was all. Time had passed, and we were still broken up, here on this beach and everywhere else.

*Time is an idiot*, I thought, as I was seized by a tremendous sense of powerlessness.

Yukihiko and I, we were like idiots. Everyone – we were all idiots, I thought, as I wrapped my arms even tighter around Yukihiko's waist.

'Why is it that we can't make it work, even though we love each other?' I asked, even though I knew that the answer didn't matter.

'It's because I'm helpless,' Yukihiko replied quietly.

'Helpless?'

Yukihiko was silent for a moment. Then he said, 'Kanoko, I really loved you.'

The tide had come in, and our legs were wet. I wondered how long the driftwood we were sitting on had been there. It must have always been in the same spot, without being swept away, even when the ocean was rough and the waves were high.

Yukihiko and I too lingered, unmoving in the night, like something that had been on this beach for a long time. I could feel Yukihiko's heartbeat reverberating throughout his entire body. I wondered if that tiny crab had made it back to its hole.

'It's getting cold, Yukihiko.'

'Let's stay like this a little longer.'

'Nuh-uh, let's go back to the inn,' I said slowly. My mind was still a blank.

'Is that a good idea?'

'Let's go back to the inn, and go to bed like a good boy and girl.'

Yukihiko laughed. He patted my head. *Yukihiko*, I murmured his name. Deep in my heart.

'Let's stay like this a little longer,' Yukihiko said.

'Okay.' I nodded.

'The lights offshore are pretty,' I said, in a blank voice.

'They are pretty,' Yukihiko agreed.

'I wish the night tide would just keep coming in forever.'

I wished the night tide would come in, and we'd be submerged, and then we'd turn into tiny crabs. And once we became crabs – without knowing about one another – when the tide went out, we'd come out of our holes, and when it came in, we'd return.

Now I could feel Yukihiko's heartbeat reverberating throughout my entire body.

'Yukihiko,' I said out loud. I tried to condense all of the kindness I felt at that moment into my voice.

'Huh?'

'Yukihiko,' I said again. This time as quietly as I could, keeping my tone neutral.

'Huh?'

Ever so quietly, traces of Yukihiko and of me spread out towards the night tide.

'Yukihiko.' I said his name one more time. This time I made no sound at all.

*Yukihiko. It's a shame we can't go back. Yukihiko. Time goes on, and I'm lonely. Yukihiko. We were idiots, weren't we?*

Every so often the waves made a crashing sound, and then would recede. The tide came in even further. In the night, my heart was racing, on and on, forever.

# The Kingdom at Summer's End

It was summer.

*I'd really like to have sex with him,* I thought.

This always happened. When I looked at a boy (no matter how much older they might be, any man who aroused lust in me would always be considered a 'boy'), the first thought that entered my mind was almost never, *I could fall in love with someone like him.* My first thought was likely to be something much more matter-of-fact – such as, *I want him to wrap his arms around the nape of my neck,* or *I'd like to tear a fresh-baked loaf of bread in half and devour it with him,* or *I'd like to take his fingers in my mouth.*

In Nishino's case, frankly, what I thought was, *I'd like to have sex with him.*

So I told him.

'Hey, let's do it,' I said.

'Where?' Nishino asked in reply. I thought it was notable

that he didn't ask, Do what?

'Do you live alone, Nishino?' I asked.

'I've been on my own since I went to university,' Nishino replied. 'All alone, for more than ten years now.'

Before going to Nishino's apartment, I bought a toothbrush and a change of underwear at a convenience store. When I came over to where Nishino was standing, flipping through a magazine, he grinned at me.

'Are you staying over?' Nishino asked.

'I have what I need to stay over, but if you don't want me to, I won't.'

'Hmm,' Nishino muttered. 'But if you don't stay over, then the toothbrush and underwear will go to waste.'

'I can take them home, so it's fine,' I replied. 'I go through, like, a toothbrush a week. I brush really hard.'

'You go through toothbrushes, do you?' Nishino had started walking, and he laughed as he spoke. 'Does that mean you go through underwear as quickly too, Sunaga?' Nishino had taken my hand.

'You can call me Reiko,' I said, squeezing his hand in return.

'Reiko, dear. Reiko. Rei,' Nishino murmured, as though he were testing these out. 'Rei is good, right? It gives the sense of your whole person, and it suits you too.' Nishino touched the top of my head. My hair was stiff, and the whorl at the back of my head stood straight up. Even though I had done my best to smooth over it with my pixie cut.

'I like the nape of your neck, Rei,' Nishino said. And then he quickened his step. Nishino's entire body exuded a sense of anticipation. That itself made me incredibly happy. *Hurry up, I want it*, I recited to myself, as I broke into a little trot to keep up with him. Beads of sweat trickled down the backs of both my and Nishino's neck.

'Ah,' Nishino said.

Dressed neatly in a suit, Nishino cut a handsome figure. *I see*, I thought to myself, impressed. *This is a guy who operates squarely within society*. I was impressed, because here I was, half-naked, tightly embracing him. Inside his front door. It was the next morning.

'It must have fallen somewhere,' Nishino said, gently peeling my body off him.

'What?' I asked.

'The key.'

'Whose key?'

Nishino didn't reply. He had stooped down and was fumbling around on the concrete floor of the entryway.

'The one from my last girlfriend,' Nishino said, after searching for a bit longer.

'Your last one?' I asked.

'The last one. Or rather, the girlfriend I'm in the process of breaking up with.'

'The girlfriend you're in the process of breaking up with? Sounds complicated,' I murmured, and Nishino nodded his head subtly. He kept looking even as he nodded.

'Since we are breaking up, I thought she must have given it back . . . Surely.'

It was the way he said 'surely' that made Nishino seem like he was a square.

'Hey, I can look for it for you. It's just a normal key, right?' I asked. Nishino stood up.

'Okay, if you don't mind.' He hurriedly opened the door and rushed out into the hallway.

Now that he was gone, I sat down on the ledge by the front door and reflected upon Nishino's body. Having sex with Nishino had been kind of great. Not fantastic. But still kind of great.

'He acts cool, but then he also seems like a hard worker,' I muttered. There it was. I had a good feeling about Nishino. This guy who acted cool, but who was a surprisingly hard worker.

I found the key. It was a pretty key, shiny and silver. Seemed like it had hardly been used. I tried to imagine just what kind of girl would suit Nishino well. What kind of hair. What kind of face. How tall. How she would talk. How she would move. What kind of personality. I considered each of these things.

It was a habit of mine. This speculation wasn't because I had fallen in love with Nishino. It was more likely due to the nature of my job. I made a living from writing novels – ones that were not quite for children and not quite for grown-ups. My books didn't sell all that well, but well enough that I could live on my own without being impoverished.

Once I had thoroughly worked out all the particulars of 'a girl who would suit Nishino', I put the key on the dining table and slipped back into Nishino's bed. I pulled a novel from Nishino's shelves – *The Broken Commandment* by Toson Shimazaki – and leafed through it. In addition to *The Broken Commandment*, Nishino's bookshelves contained

*Pregnant Fiction* by Minako Saito and *The World According to Garp* by John Irving, along with several new-looking business-related books.

*This boy is not easy to pin down*, I thought to myself as I opened *The Broken Commandment* at the beginning and gazed at the words on the page.

At some point I fell asleep. Nestled in the sheets that still smelled of Nishino's and my skin from the night before, and with *The Broken Commandment* still in my hand, I drifted in and out of a light slumber.


Nishino didn't come home from the office until after eleven o'clock that night. When he saw me sitting at the dining table with my laptop computer open, he looked momentarily surprised, but his expression quickly regained its composure. Nothing seemed to disturb Nishino's placidity.

'Welcome home,' I ventured.

He uttered some kind of sound in response. I asked him to clarify what that sound meant – I usually say whatever is in my head.

'Well, what would you like me to say?' Nishino asked, sounding a little bit baffled.

'Most people would be upset when a woman they've had sex with just once settles in to stay.'

'Ah.'

'That's what I mean – "Ah" is not much of a response!'

'Ah.'

Now Nishino seemed truly lost. He must have been tired. If I had to leave the house before eight in the morning and work all day, not getting home until eleven at night, I'd collapse after a day or two. It was understandable.

'If I'm bothering you – really, just say so,' I shut off my computer and closed it. A light breeze billowed the curtains, ever so slightly. You would think that by this time it would have cooled off a bit but, even late at night, the Tokyo summer air was still heavy, laden with humidity.

'Should I turn on the air conditioning?' I ventured.

'Ah,' Nishino replied, with the same tone. I shut the window, firmly adjusting the curtain, and switched it on, using the remote control. The hum of the air conditioner started up abruptly. Nishino stared idly at the ceiling as he loosened his tie with one hand, took off his shirt, neatly hung his trousers on a hanger and then headed for the bathroom. He moved as if he were an automated doll.

'I'll take a bath with you,' I said, and Nishino nodded mildly.

'It's not bothersome to go in together?' I hazarded to ask, since Nishino's expression was as vague as ever.

'What do you mean, "bothersome"?'

'What do you mean, "what do you mean"?'

'Rei, you're kind of like an animal, aren't you?'

*Me, an animal?* I thought. But from my perspective, it was Nishino who seemed more like an animal. If he wanted to seem more human, he'd need to exhibit more human actions and statements.

Nishino ran the hot water, dutifully scrubbing down the bath with a sponge before filling it.

'Why don't you go first, Rei?' Nishino said as he sank into the sofa, now wearing only his briefs and undershirt.

'Let's take one together,' I reiterated. 'We can wash each other, scrub each other's backs, massage the pressure points on each other's feet.'

Nishino smiled with a sense of reticence.

'It's cramped in there, so I think you'll be more comfortable if you go in alone,' Nishino said.

'Bathing alone is boring,' I replied. 'I've been here on my own all day long. Now that you're home, I thought we could take a bath together.'

'No, I prefer to bathe by myself,' Nishino said in a shy voice.

'See, now, you should have said so before!'

'Huh?'

'Things are much easier when you say what you really think.'

'Just like you do, Rei.'

'Yup,' I replied as I opened the door to the bathroom. Most people can't actually say exactly what they really think – but I still didn't understand why everyone always shied away from speaking even a fraction of what was in their head. I mean, it's not as if you're going to be punished just for saying one or even two per cent of what you're thinking.

I immersed myself in the hot water, curling my body into a ball. I heated up right away, so I washed myself and my hair perfunctorily, then dunked myself in the bath once more, and hurriedly left the bathroom.

'That was really fast,' Nishino said, widening his eyes. 'I thought all girls took long baths.'

'I'm not such a fan of baths.'

'Is that so?' Nishino murmured. 'How old are you again,

Rei? Are you about the same age as me, around thirty?' He asked, his tone noncommittal.

'I'm older than you are.'

'Hmm,' Nishino said. He didn't question me any further. Though I wouldn't have minded if he had. Maybe he was uninterested. Or maybe he figured that all women were distressed about their age.

'Do you mind if I have a beer?' I asked.

'Go ahead.'

'Should we share it?'

'Ah,' Nishino replied, somewhat more forcefully than he had before. This 'ah' contained within it Nishino's own volition, the first I had heard since he had come home.

'Hurry up and take your bath. I'll wait for you,' I said, unravelling the towel from around my head and waving it like a flag. Nishino headed towards the bathroom, shedding his briefs and undershirt. He let out an audible sigh as he stretched. I heard the bathroom door close.

Nishino took a long time in the bath. The can of beer I had taken out was gradually losing its chill so I put it back in the refrigerator. I must have fallen asleep, sprawled diagonally on the sofa. The next thing I knew, droplets of water were trickling down onto me from Nishino just above me, as he pulled out the towel that was twisted around my body. My eyes opened and met his, 'Come on in,' I said, and he chuckled.

We had sex, briefly. Not fantastic, but kind of great sex. After we had finished, as promised, we drank a beer together. The can had rechilled, and was nice and frosty. I drank mine down in one go. Nishino stared at me as I tossed it back.

'Are you staying over tonight too, Rei?' Nishino asked.

'I'm not sure . . . I don't have any deadlines at the moment, so I could stay,' I said, and Nishino nodded. Then he ruffled my hair, tousling it right at the spot on top of my head where it stood up straight.


I was at Nishino's apartment for five days. Friday was usually when I received a fax with corrections to my manuscript, so after I'd seen Nishino off to work, I gathered my things (the underwear that I had washed three times, the toothbrush that was already half frayed and the laptop that I always carried with me), quickly swept the apartment and locked the door behind me. I tossed the key back through the newspaper box on the door, and headed for my own apartment.

Once I had boarded the train that I hadn't ridden for a while, my time at Nishino's apartment began to feel like something from the distant past. Regardless of how clearly I could recall the days I had spent there. Nishino's body, Nishino's gaze, Nishino's words. Yet the moment I was no longer there, all of it became distant somehow.

The cicadas were buzzing. There had been hardly any cicadas near Nishino's apartment. Leaving the windows open had only allowed the hot air from the other apartments' air conditioners to pour into Nishino's, so eventually I had stopped bothering to open them. Despite the fact that I hated air conditioning, I had ended up just leaving it on at Nishino's.

When I got home, I threw open the windows and curtains and filled my ears with the sound of the cicadas. Besides the fax with the corrections, two others had come in. A request to review a children's book, and a pamphlet-length questionnaire from a life insurance company.

*Do you experience anxiety about your retirement?*
*What do you imagine when you hear the words 'your future'?*

'The future, indeed,' I muttered to myself as I crumpled up the life insurance fax and threw it in the bin.

I went through the corrections carefully and faxed them back, then read over the materials for the manuscript that was due at the end of the following week. After a late lunch, I was feeling drowsy. In summertime, I pull a huge *goza* mat made of rushes out from the back of the cupboard and leave it on the tatami floor. I laid down on the mat and promptly fell asleep.

When I awoke, it was completely dark. I felt energized. *Maybe I should call someone and go out tonight,* I had just thought to myself when the phone rang.

'Ah, Rei.'

I didn't immediately recognize who it was.

'Uh-huh,' I mumbled in reply.

'I'm glad you're there.'

'I'm here. My place after all,' I said, and the person laughed. It was by the laugh that I realized it was Nishino.

'How are you?' I asked.

'I was surprised to come home and not find you here.'

'I had work to do,' I replied, and Nishino laughed again.

'It's a tough world when even animals have to work,' he said.

'It's hot, isn't it? Wherever you go. Want to go out for

a beer?' I ventured. I had been with Nishino up until this morning, so I had been in the mood to get together with another friend, but here he was on the phone. I figured that inviting him was the polite thing to do.

'Sure,' Nishino said. There was a note of politeness in his voice too. Politeness begat politeness, I guessed. There was something strange, I thought, about the way that Nishino must have used this same voice with every girl. He appeared so cool, and here he was, such an unexpectedly diligent worker.

'Hey, what do you imagine when you hear the words "the future"?' I decided to ask.

'Why do you ask, out of the blue?'

'I'm talking about the future.'

'Hmm ...' Nishino murmured for a moment. He had probably gone straight to the idea of being made to commit. Things that were connected with marriage, or family.

'Me, I think of castle walls.'

Nishino was just humming away without any sort of response, so I had offered my own first.

'Castle walls?' Nishino asked.

'Like in a kingdom.'

'A kingdom.'

'Yeah – a kingdom where it's always summer, there are lots of cicadas buzzing and it's surrounded by high castle walls and ruled fairly by a very old king.'

'Th ... that's your image of the future, Rei?' I could sense Nishino's confusion over the phone.

'Right.'

'But then, in your mind, how are the cicadas related to that old king?'

'Doesn't a kingdom like that seem like a happy place to live?' I said. Nishino sighed.

'I don't get it. In your version of the future, there's nothing like marriage, or children, or pensions.'

'No, there isn't. Not even if you look at it sideways or turn it upside down.' That was how I really felt, and I said so.

'Well, anyway, should we go for a beer?' I asked, and Nishino agreed, sounding relieved.

I was kind of beginning to like Nishino. I realized this as I was getting ready to go out. Just beginning to like him, not totally in love. *Next week, after my deadline, I should go out with someone else, not Nishino*, I thought to myself, as I slid my heels into the straps of my sandals.


Nishino said that he had 'properly' returned his key to his 'last girlfriend'. He seemed to insert this casually into a pause in our conversation.

But I could tell that it wasn't really so casual. Nishino wanted to be sure to tell me. This was the kind of thing that irritated me. If Nishino liked me, why not just say so? As far as I was concerned, telling me that he had given his old girlfriend her key back was not any sort of metaphor and had no implication.

'Are you busy at work?' I asked in a perfunctory manner. I was rapidly losing interest in Nishino.

'No busier than usual,' Nishino replied easily.

*I'll have one more glass, and then go home*, I decided.

'Oh, crap!' I said. 'I forgot all about a deadline I have.'

I wasn't so inundated with requests that I would forget a deadline. But Nishino wouldn't know that.

'Oh, really?' Nishino looked at me with a smile on his face that implied plenty of assurance. 'Hey, what's your apartment like, Rei?' Nishino asked.

'Nothing special. I have one room with tatami mats and one room with a wooden floor, and the walls of both are lined with bookcases. Other than that, I have a small television, a medium-sized refrigerator and a fax machine.'

'Sounds just like the kind of apartment you'd have, Rei.' Nishino smiled. He was the type of guy who looked good when he smiled. His appearance was neat, and though there was a hint of an edge about him, he spoke without a trace of sarcasm. Why had I slept with a boy like this, one who would be just fine for any kind of girl? I regretted it.

'Well, then, I'll be going.' I stood up as I drained the alcohol that was left in my glass.

Nishino was momentarily blank. Then he quickly regained his composure. The thing was, if he were to remain blank like that, I might actually be more interested in him. I thought this to myself and gave a little wave to Nishino as he sat there. I pressed a 5,000-yen note into his palm, and hurriedly started walking towards the door.

I took long and deep breaths as I walked along the street to the station. After I'd walked for a bit, I completely forgot about Nishino.


Nishino went on, 'But, Rei, maybe you don't like me all that much.'

It had been around three weeks since I'd last spoken to Nishino. I'd had an unusual convergence of deadlines, and also I'd had to go to the Kansai region to do some research. He called me on Sunday evening, when I had just returned from my trip. Alone in my apartment, I had hastily put away my bags and was excitedly preparing some saké to go with the mackerel sushi I had splurged on – this *sabazushi* was especially fancy and I was looking forward to polishing it off.

Nishino called me saying that he missed me at the exact moment when the saké I was heating up was at just the right temperature.

'Right, yeah, maybe we can see each other next week,' I replied vaguely, more focused on the saké.

'Come on, aren't you free tonight?' Nishino persisted.

'It's urgent?' I asked brusquely.

'Nothing in particular. It's just that I haven't seen you all this time, and I guess I'm bored,' Nishino said. 'I miss you. I want to see your face, Rei. I want to talk to you.' Nishino went on, 'But, Rei, maybe you don't like me all that much.'

*Huh? Wait a minute*, I thought. Could Nishino really be so upfront?

This was not the Nishino I was used to. Unlike before, when my interest in Nishino had suddenly waned, now my curiosity was just as suddenly piqued.

'Rei, it's just that, I really need to be with someone now,' Nishino said.

'But, Nishino, you have lots of girlfriends and lovers, don't you? Isn't that your thing, knowing all about girls?' I asked. Nishino made a sound in the back of his throat.

'Why would you say that to me, Rei?'

'But, I really thought it was your speciality.'

'Well, maybe I am like one of those guys – you know, a womanizer. But how do you know about that, Rei? I haven't said a word to you about my love affairs or about my recent sex life.'

'I can tell, from talking to you and from having sex with you – that's all it takes,' I replied, laughing.

Nishino laughed too, on the other end of the line. It was the most cheerful I had ever heard his laughter sound.

*Nishino – he's not so bad. In fact, he's kind of great*, I thought to myself.

'Hey, Nishino, I've just brought back some *sabazushi* from Kyoto today. It cost me 5,000 yen. We can eat it together.' The moment the idea occurred to me, I said it. 'But if you want some, you have to come right over. Otherwise I'll eat it all myself.'

Nishino laughed again cheerfully.

'Do you mind if I bring underwear and a toothbrush?' Nishino asked. 'So that I can stay over, as long as you don't mind.'

'And if I do mind, what will you do with them?' I ventured.

'Then I'll donate the toothbrush to you.'

'And what will you do with the underwear?'

'I will dejectedly take it home with me.'

'Enough – just bring your suit for tomorrow,' I said.

While I waited for Nishino to arrive, I pulled the guest bedding from the cupboard – the bottom futon and the coverlet, sheets and a pillow cover – and laid them out in the tatami room. It had been a long time since I'd had a boy over to my apartment. When I felt like having sex, I went right ahead and slept with a boy, but that isn't to say that my desire was unremitting. It had been more than three years since a boy had come and gone from this apartment.

'Nishino.' I tried saying his name out loud. I was definitely looking forward to his visit.

'Nishino.' I tried saying it aloud once more. I wanted to fall in love with him. If only I could fall in love with him. Without realizing it, that was what I was hoping for.

I loved the idea of falling in love with someone, but the actual being in love part was difficult. I was all too familiar with my own desires. And I was very straightforward about asking myself what it was that I really wanted.

'If only I could want all of Nishino,' I murmured.

I took three aubergines out of the refrigerator. I pierced the skin of the aubergines with a fork, and arranged them on the grill, lighting the flame on the gas stove. At first the flame was orange, but soon it changed to a pretty blue.

For a while, I stared intently at the transparent blue flame of the gas.


It was summer's end when I began to fall in love with Nishino.

I truly wanted all of him now.

That day, before we ate the grilled aubergines, Nishino and I had sex. Tenderly, gently. By the time we had finished, I was no longer evaluating what having sex with Nishino was like. What I mean is, without worrying about whether the sex was kind of great, or fantastic, it just got better.

Once I've decided that I'm in love with all of someone – once I stop making value judgements about this thing being good or that being bad – it gets better. I can just be in love.

This is why, ever since that day at the end of summer, sex with Nishino became simply 'sex with someone I love'. No longer 'kind of great sex with someone' or 'fantastic sex with someone'.

'I want all of you.'

Nishino had nodded when I said that, after we had sex that day. I doubt that Nishino understood – at that time or even afterwards – what I meant by 'all of you'. After all, Nishino didn't know what it was really like to fall in love with a girl – he never tried to figure it out – because he was a boy.

'How do you know I'm like one of those guys?' Nishino probably would have asked, if I had voiced what I was thinking.

And wouldn't I have responded the same way? 'I can tell, from talking to you and from having sex with you – that's all it takes.'

The trouble with wanting all of a boy like Nishino was that it was predictable. Of course, even after I decided on all of him, Nishino thought nothing of sleeping with girls who weren't me. He slept with younger girls and older girls. With girls who were crazy in love with him and with girls who were just having fun, no strings attached. All I had to do was take a good hard look at Nishino, and I could tell as much.

But I paid no mind – I loved Nishino a lot.

I simply loved him.

There was only the smallest part of me that wanted to

be loved (not even I could manage to love someone without hoping for a smidgen of love in return).

'Summer will be over soon, you know,' I said. It had been about a year since I had started loving Nishino.

'You're right,' Nishino said. We were lying next to each other and he was stroking the top of my head.

'I've always liked summer's end,' I murmured.

'Me, I've never really liked it,' Nishino replied flatly.

All I could do was sputter in response.

A sense of discomfort. I don't think I ever called it that. But, the entire time I was in love with Nishino, I always felt a bit unsettled. A small but concentrated and stubbornly persistent ache, like a knot.

'My sister died at the end of summer,' Nishino told me softly that day.

'Really?' I whispered. It was the first time he had mentioned it. Nishino hardly ever talked about himself.

Tentatively, I stroked the top of Nishino's head.

'While I was on my way to stay at a friend's beach house, my sister killed herself by taking poison, in a nearby field. If only I had been home, I would have noticed. But I had gone to the beach house.' Nishino spoke in the same monotone as always.

'When they found her, it was too late. My sister was dead.'

I continued stroking Nishino's head attentively. He didn't say anything more. I remained silent.

For the first time since falling in love with Nishino, I began to doubt him.

Maybe Nishino was incapable of love.

This had never occurred to me – not when he thought nothing of sleeping with other girls, not when I caught him telling little white lies.

Something like cool air seemed to emanate from Nishino's body. The truth was, before he told me about his sister's suicide, that chill must have always been present, like a thin, sharp wisp. But I had pretended not to notice it. I hadn't even been aware of my own effort.

*Such profound depths this poor guy has*, I thought, forlornly.

'Nishino.' I called his name.

'What is it, Rei?'

'I love you. I loved you.'

'What?' Nishino's eyes widened. 'Why did you use the past tense?'

'Because I can't love you any more,' I told him honestly. I couldn't say it any other way.

'Why?' Nishino sat up. I gazed sadly at the taut muscles in his stomach and chest.

'I'm sorry.'

'Is it because I wasn't faithful?' Nishino asked.

'Maybe . . .' I replied. But I knew very well that it wasn't.

'I'm sorry. I won't sleep with other girls any more. I promise I won't!' Nishino cried out.

I was startled. I hadn't thought that he cared enough about me to shout like that. I had assumed he cared a little. But I knew that he wasn't crazy in love with me.

'I loved you,' I repeated. Just as forlornly as before.

'Rei, is it really too late? Come on, how can it be?'

Nishino was crying.

'I didn't know how much I loved you, Rei,' he said through his tears.

'I love you, Rei.'

'I'm sorry,' I said firmly.

Deep in my heart, I wondered whether a girl existed in the world who was kind and strong enough to love Nishino. Perhaps. It was unlikely.

I felt sorry for Nishino, and almost started crying. But I steeled myself. At the same time, I remembered the cool air that had emanated from Nishino just before, and I shivered for real.

I wanted to flee from Nishino as quickly as possible. This desire welled up from the bottom of my heart. I still couldn't put my finger on what that sense of discomfort was – all I knew for sure was that it was present. And no matter how hard I tried, I simply couldn't make it go away – that cold and awful uneasiness.

I wanted to flee. This simple thought flooded my mind. The same way that I had wished I could love him.


'Goodbye,' Nishino said for the last time. His tone was polite and kind.

*Oh, will the poor guy spend his life alone like this?* I wondered, as I looked Nishino straight in the eyes.

'Someday, I hope you'll show me the kingdom at summer's end,' Nishino said. He was smiling.

'Oh, someday. Someday when I'm older, when I'm tougher, when I'm stronger,' I said, hanging my head.

'Goodbye,' Nishino said once more.

'Goodbye,' I said back to him.

We had walked along the street that leads from my apartment to the station. On this day that would be our last, Nishino had come to my place to get his things. I had kept hardly anything of mine at Nishino's apartment. A half-worn toothbrush and three spare ones. I gave the extra ones to Nishino and asked him to throw away the half-worn one.

'You know, I have the feeling that I'll die at the end of summer,' Nishino said, looking up.

'Then I'll have to show you the kingdom before then.'

'Well, then I'll live a long life, and wait for you to toughen up.'

'Think I ever will?'

'I doubt it. You'll always be like a little animal, after all, Rei.'

Nishino smiled. There was something odd about his smile, as if he knew perfectly well that no woman could truly love him. His smile reminded me of the transparent blue flame of the gas burner on the stove.

I was on the verge of tears. I was so close to telling Nishino that I wanted to love him again. But I couldn't bring myself to say it.

'Take care of yourself, Nishino.' I stopped walking.

'You too, Rei, take care.' Nishino hurried through the ticket gate and was gone. He didn't look back.

I watched Nishino until he disappeared from sight. When I happened to look down at my feet, a cicada was lying there, belly-up. I nudged it gently with the tip of my shoe, and the cicada moved slightly.

Soon it started to buzz.

As I was watching, the cicada's drone grew louder. When I nudged it once more with my toe, it quivered its wings and took off in flight.

The cicada flew up into the sky. The faint hum of its wings lingered in my ears.

# Osaka Tower

Subaru has the softest hair.

I loved to play with Subaru's hair. But Subaru told me she hated to have her hair touched. No matter who the one touching it was. Like, she wouldn't even want the person she loved the most in this world to softly caress her hair, she declared. Subaru tended to make declarations very easily.

But I knew better. There was one time when Nishino was stroking Subaru's hair, and I heard a faint sound coming from deep in Subaru's throat. It sounded like a cat purring with pleasure. And like a cat, Subaru stretched out her back as she sat on the floor. Nishino shifted his caress to her back in one long stroke, even reaching her buttocks. Then he kissed her lightly and heaved himself to his feet.

'Nishinooo!' Subaru called out. The way she said his name sounded like a word in a foreign language. Whenever she called him, she always drew out the end of his name. Her inflection could have been taken either as an endearment or an insult.

'You're leaving?' Subara asked.

'Uh-huh,' Nishino replied. And then, in the direction of where I was hiding behind the refrigerator, he said, 'And, you, don't just sit there, listening attentively – show yourself!'

For some reason, the refrigerator in the apartment Subaru and I shared was not against a wall. Instead, it was smack in the middle of the room. Subaru had moved it there at one point, saying that it was nice to have the fridge within arm's reach at all times.

Nishino soon left. Subaru was still lying on the floor. Dust motes were floating in the sunlight that shone through the window. But you couldn't see any beyond where the light fell. Subaru faced the sunbeam and, still lying down, reached her hand out to it. She balled her hand into a fist, as if trying to grab the motes.

'Can't catch them,' Subaru said from her prone position.

'They call it the Tyndall effect,' I said in a quiet voice.

'The "tin" what?'

'It's what makes the dust motes look like they're floating like that.'

'How do you know these things, Tama?' Subaru asked, lifting herself up sideways on one elbow.

'I learned about it from Nishino,' I said even more quietly. Subaru opened the refrigerator door with her foot, stuck her delicate toes inside for a moment and then closed it. The fridge made a humming sound.

'That's great,' Subaru said loudly. She pronounced each syllable with the same emphasis, making the words seem like a sticky orb.

'Nishino knows about all kinds of things, surprisingly,'

I said, to which Subaru uttered her gooey 'That's great' once more. I stood up, and Subaru then did a somersault. A small tumble. Subaru was very flexible, so she could manage to do a somersault in even the tightest spaces. Her face held a sullen expression as she rolled around. She must have been angry that Nishino hadn't given her a proper kiss goodbye. And maybe also that it had been me and not her who knew about that 'tin' whatever it was.

I had got to know Nishino a little while back. That is, when Subaru dragged him back here. She had met Nishino in a bar somewhere, and they had talked together for hours. Ultimately, she had brought him back to the apartment.

'She said she was sleee-py,' Nishino had explained to me in a mild tone, that day. As proof of her own words, Subaru was now lying on the floor like a puddle of water, fast asleep.

'I've never heard a girl say that so sleepily,' Nishino said with a laugh.

'Subaru is nothing if not straightforward,' I replied bluntly. I was annoyed with both Subaru, who had randomly brought home some guy she didn't know, and with the guy himself, who seemed to have no reservations about coming over to someone's apartment – particularly when he didn't seem all that intent on having sex with her. I don't respond well to unclear situations.

'Things have to be either black or white for Tama,' Subaru liked to say.

'No, they can also be red or green, yellow or purple – there are lots of options,' I would reply, and Subaru would laugh out loud. Subaru's voice was clear and pure. As I thought of her carelessly telling a guy she barely knew in that clear voice, 'I'm sleee-py,' I got more and more irritated.

'Want something to drink?' Nishino had asked me at the time, his gaze fixed on Subaru sleeping on the floor.

'Nothing for me,' I replied instantly. 'And this is our apartment, anyway,' I went on pointedly.

Nishino narrowed his eyes. 'You must be Tama, dear?'

'Are you the kind of guy who calls every girl "dear"?' I spat out, glaring at him.

Nishino was not the least bit put out; he reached into his bag and pulled out a can of oolong tea.

'Not all of them,' Nishino said, as he opened the pull tab. 'Only girls like you, Tama, dear, whom it seems to suit.' The can was at an angle, so a little of the oolong tea spilled out. I wanted to slap him in the face.

'It's almost time for tomorrow. Hurry home now,' I said, pointing towards the front door. It's bad manners to point, Subaru would have told me. She was oddly old-fashioned about certain things.

'Time for tomorrow – that's a nice way of putting it,' Nishino said, as he stood and, drinking his oolong tea, put on his shoes by the front door. He pushed open the door with the hand that was holding his bag and, continuing to drink his tea, he went outside. Then he clomped down the stairs.

The slice of sky carved out in the height of the front door was ever so slightly brightening. A coolness rose from around my feet.

'It's definitely time for tomorrow,' I murmured. Even

though tomorrow actually began at midnight, I always felt as though the wee hours, until dawn, still belonged to yesterday. But that too was all over once it was daylight. Most people wouldn't deny that tomorrow arrived with the dawn.

I hurried to close the front door, and took some apple juice out of the refrigerator. The juice was in a tall plastic container; I poured a glass half full, sipping it slowly.

*Subaru must really like this Nishino fellow*, I thought to myself. The refrigerator hummed. Subaru stirred a bit. While I covered her with a blanket, I gently caressed her cheek. She couldn't complain about it if she was sleeping.


After that, Nishino started coming by frequently. He would just show up without any notice.

'Nishino, don't you have the courtesy to do something like call beforehand?' I asked.

'I hate the anticipation when I've been forewarned,' Subaru interjected. Nishino simply smiled.

Since he came by without warning, often I would be the only one at the apartment. Subaru had always liked going out to wander.

'Tama, dear, how come you're always in a ball?' Nishino asked me once. When I was at home, I was usually curled up on the rug. Subaru would say that I was exhausted from trying to make everything black or white, out in the world.

'I feel safe when I'm curled up in a ball.'

'Subaru is always sprawled out.'

'Because she's straightforward, like I said before.'

'Girls who are straightforward sprawl out?'

'Finicky ones curl up, and straightforward ones stretch out.'

'Tama, dear, you're kind of strange,' Nishino said, seemingly impressed. 'Say, how old are you, Tama, dear?'

'Same age as Subaru. Twenty-one.'

'Eh?' Nishino expressed surprise.

'The year I was born, that truck driver, Mr Onuki, found one hundred million yen on the street in Ginza, and when I was four years old, the Mystery Man with Twenty-One Faces was on a crime spree.' As I explained this, Nishino was staring fixedly at my face.

'Think I look old for my age?'

'No, Tama, dear, you look like you could be ten or twenty or seventy.'

'What's that supposed to mean?' I asked, throwing a cushion at Nishino. He caught it with both hands and then buried his face in it.

'Smells good. Must be your smell, Tama, dear,' he said, or something to that effect.

'When Subaru and I first met, we got all worked up talking about what we would do with a hundred million yen,' I said quickly, averting my gaze from Nishino, who was playing with the cushion.

'What would you do?' Nishino asked.

'I would bury it in the ground, and dig it up every so often, just to grin at it.'

'A sound plan.'

'Yup.'

'What did Subaru say she'd do with it?'

'Get this – she said she'd buy a dog and a dog house and a dog collar.'

'That wouldn't cost a hundred million yen.'

'I guess she would get a really lavish dog collar, encrusted with diamonds and emeralds and rubies.'

'It would get stolen right away.'

'Right. Of course, it being stolen is all part of her plan.'

'What would she do after it was stolen?'

'She said she would hurl abuse at the thief and curse them with everything she'd got.'

Nishino widened his eyes. Then he gave a little laugh. 'A hundred million yen's worth of abuse, huh? That's rich.'

'And then, she said she would still have the dog and would enjoy her time living with it.'

'Hmm,' Nishino said. This time he narrowed his eyes.

'I've already decided where I would bury the hundred million yen, and Subaru knows which shop she would order the lavish dog collar from.'

'So then, all that's left is to find the hundred million yen?' Nishino chuckled.

I immediately regretted chattering away to Nishino about our silly fantasy. Sullen now, I stopped talking and curled up again on the rug.

'If I had a hundred million yen . . .' Nishino murmured. 'If I had a hundred million yen, I would spend it on making the girls I know happy,' he continued to muse.

Nishino left a little while after that.

'You know, you can't buy girls' happiness,' I griped to Nishino, once he was gone. 'The only thing that can make them happy is themselves.' Hmph.

I picked up the cushion that Nishino had buried his face in and smelled it. All I could smell was the scent of cushion. I curled up on the floor, but I couldn't relax. I tried curling up even tighter, so that my nose reached my knees. Before long, I started to feel tired, so I shifted my nose away from my knees, stretching out my limbs, loosening up a tiny bit. Then I fell asleep.

'Say, how old are you, Nishino?' I tried asking the next time he came over. Subaru was watching the television that was in a corner of the apartment. Subaru liked television. She left it on all day long. For Subaru, who didn't own a mobile phone, a television was her only luxury.

'Thirty-one. The year I was born, the Yodogo hijacking took place, and when I was four years old, that spoon-bending kid, Jun Sekiguchi, made an appearance.'

'What are you, ancient or something?' I asked Nishino. 'What is this "Yodogo" thing?'

'I drove myself crazy trying to bend spoons,' Nishino muttered wistfully, without replying to my question.

'Sometimes Subaru bends spoons,' I said, and Nishino widened his eyes. When he did this, his brow hung down, and it made his face look kind of goofy.

'She bends them very easily when she's angry. She breaks glasses too. And kicks over chairs,' I went on, and Nishino giggled.

'Subaru really is straightforward, isn't she?' Whether Subaru could hear our conversation or not, she kept her back turned and her gaze fixed on the television.

'You don't call Subaru "dear"?' I asked.

Nishino shook his head. 'It doesn't suit her.'

Something about this comment made me indignant. In addition to the fact that I saw nothing good about being a girl who was suited to being called 'dear', it angered me to be told that it did not suit Subaru. Everything in the world suited Subaru. Nishino just didn't understand. I went over to the rug and curled up on it. The sound of the weather forecast came through muffled. Subaru was especially fond of the weather forecast, so she always turned up the volume when it came on. Heavy snow was falling in the vicinity of Sekigahara. In the northern mountains, an accumulation of thirty to fifty centimetres was expected. Near the coast, the waves would be high. Anyone venturing out in this weather should take great care.

Nishino gazed at Subaru listening attentively to the weather forecast.

*If it snowed here, we should make a snowman. Just Subaru and me*, I thought, pressing my ear hard against the rug.


'How do you two support yourselves?' Nishino asked Subaru.

'We manage,' Subaru replied.

'That's not an answer,' Nishino laughed.

'Part-time jobs,' I offered instead. 'Subaru works at Shima, and I work here and there.'

Shima was the bar where Subaru helped out about four times a week. It was a Spanish *izakaya* named after the owner, Mr Shima, a middle-aged guy who ran it by himself.

'What makes it Spanish?' I once asked Subaru.

'Seems like he just throws garlic into every dish,' she replied.

Mr Shima had been Subaru's lover at one point. He had even come over to our apartment, but just once.

'Wow, this place is cramped – both of you girls live here?' Mr Shima had said, as he surveyed the apartment.

'What do you see in that guy?' I had asked Subaru after Mr Shima left.

'His legs are thick – I like that,' she had replied. 'Me, I like guys with thick arms and legs.'

Not long after that, Subaru broke up with Mr Shima, and around that time she started helping out at his bar.

'Usually it works the other way, right?' I said. You break up, and then you stop working at the guy's place, or so I thought.

Subaru had just stared at me and said, 'Never mix business with pleasure, Tama.'

'I want to save up some money. I really should,' Subaru said.

'What will you do with it once you save it?' Nishino asked.

'I'll live next to Osaka Tower,' Subaru replied, as she sipped her tea. Nishino had made black tea for her. Subaru always added plenty of warm milk to her tea.

'Why Osaka Tower?' Nishino was also sipping tea.

'Did you know that, originally, Osaka Tower was meant to combine the designs of both the Eiffel Tower and the Arc de Triomphe in Paris?' Subaru explained. She was in her element when she told this story. 'It's like the Eiffel Tower was stuck right on top of the Arc de Triomphe.'

'That's amazing,' Nishino said, impressed.

'It *was* amazing.' Subaru nodded. 'But it was destroyed in

a fire. The current Osaka Tower is the second one.'

'Why do you want to live next to Osaka Tower?' Nishino asked.

'Because it's awesome!' Subaru replied.

'Living next to Tokyo Tower would be nice too,' I said in a quiet voice, but Subaru shook her head.

'There's something sad about Tokyo Tower.'

'I guess you're right. It is sad, isn't it?' Nishino said.

*It is* not *sad. If the two of us lived there – whether it was next to Tokyo Tower or wherever – there wouldn't be anything sad about it*, I chimed in. But just in my head. Without saying a word.

*Was Nishino Subaru's lover?* This question too was ventured silently, without speaking. There was something elusive about both of them – whereas, up until now, I had been able to tell right away which guy was Subaru's lover, I was stumped when it came to Nishino.

'I can't stand it when things aren't black or white.' This phrase I mumbled out loud.

'Black and white are the same, you know,' Nishino said.

'When I go up Osaka Tower, I'm going to wear a bright white coat, with bright white boots.' Subaru spoke these words like a song.

'Subaru, you mean to tell me that you've never been up Osaka Tower?' Nishino asked.

'Nope. Never even seen it,' Subaru replied.

'Guess you'd better start saving up then,' Nishino said. I thought he was then going to offer to take her there, but he didn't. Nishino was gazing at Subaru. Subaru was gazing back at him. I alone was looking out of the window.

I felt a little pang in my chest. It was probably jealousy. But I didn't know what I was jealous of. It looked like it was going to snow. The black tea that Nishino had made for me was now completely cold.

The day Nishino told me he wanted me was particularly cold, even for that winter.

Nishino was a little drunk, which was unusual for him.

'Tama, dear, have you and Subaru ever hooked up?' Nishino asked. This was another day when Subaru was out wandering around.

'Don't ask rude questions,' I replied crossly.

'Sorry.' Nishino apologized. And then he went on, in a quiet voice, 'I want you, Tama, dear.'

I was bewildered – I had never heard anyone use that expression before. Boys didn't say that. They were much more casual about it. I stifled a giggle. There had been a few times when Subaru and I had found ourselves naked and entwined, kissing and touching each other's bodies. Perhaps if we had known better – about how to proceed as lovers, I mean – Subaru and I might have had a chance at a physical and emotional relationship, but things didn't go that way. And if they had, I know that it would have frightened me. I wondered how Subaru felt about it.

'You want, me?' I said, laughing, and Nishino enveloped me in his arms. He caressed my head. It felt good to be caressed. I wondered why Subaru hated it so much. 'Tama, dear, your hair is so smooth,' Nishino murmured. 'Subaru's hair is fluffy, you know.' The smell of alcohol drifted from above.

And just like that, we had sex on the floor. Nishino's arms were strong. Strong and thick. After we had finished, I was sad.

'Why did you do it with me?' I asked him.

'But, Tama, dear, don't you like me?' Nishino replied. His voice sounded sad. He seemed just as sad as I was.

'I wonder what makes Subaru happiest?' Nishino murmured.

'Subaru is happy no matter what she's doing,' I replied softly. But I knew that wasn't entirely true. If Subaru were to walk in here now, it would make her unhappy. She would be extremely unhappy.

'Are you and Subaru lovers?' I got up the courage to ask.

'I thought we were, but I don't know what Subaru thinks,' Nishino replied.

'Hmm,' I mumbled. Nishino raised his head. The front door had opened. I was completely still. My ear was pressed hard against the rug. There was the sound of a gasp. Nishino stood up. Subaru must have taken a step back – there was a dull thud against the door.

'Subaru,' Nishino called out. She did not reply.

'It's not what you think,' Nishino said.

'Then what is it?' Subaru asked, her voice hoarse.

'It's not what you think,' Nishino said one more time. There was the sound of the door closing, followed by the loud echo of footsteps stomping down the stairs. I shut my eyes and just kept my ear pressed against the rug.

Nishino kept standing there for a while. His legs, right before my eyes, had goosebumps from his ankles to his knees.

*What is it, then, Nishino?* In my head, I posed the same question to him. I touched Nishino's leg. He kneeled down, slowly.

'Tama, dear,' he murmured.

'Yeah,' I replied.

'Tama, dear,' Nishino whispered.

'Yeah,' I repeated. Then we held each other gently in an embrace. The refrigerator hummed.

The refrigerator was the thing that had led to Subaru and me living together.

'Someone has given me this big second-hand fridge,' Subaru had said, 'and I don't have anywhere to put it.' At the time, Subaru was living in an apartment that was even more cramped than the one we lived in now – there was almost no kitchen space to speak of.

'My refrigerator has just broken,' I told her, so the two of us ended up looking for a new apartment. We saw lots of places, but Subaru said, 'It's great!' about every one of them, leaving me to grumble about the lack of light or storage space. But the move was easy, after bringing over the refrigerator and just our few personal belongings. Both Subaru and I were poor, so we hardly had any stuff.

'Let's eat some soba noodles, to celebrate moving in,' Subaru had suggested. We went to a soba restaurant in the neighbourhood – Subaru had *okame* soba, which came with fish paste, and I had *tsukimi* soba, which came with an egg in it.

Subaru named the refrigerator Zozo.

'I wonder if it's bad karma to stick my feet inside Zozo,' Subaru would say, as she regularly opened the fridge door with her foot and stuck in her toes. No matter how often I chided her, she didn't stop.

'You're so noisy, Zozo,' she would say, and then imitate the refrigerator's humming sound. *Buunnn.*

Come to think of it, Subaru also gave the television a name. Sayoko, she called it. 'Sayoko is such a hard worker. She's glowing all day long,' Subaru would say, as she stared at Sayoko's screen, motionless. When the picture went to a snow screen, Subaru became even more fixated upon it. She would sit in front of Sayoko and say, 'I know that Osaka Tower is on the other side of that snow.'

I couldn't bring myself to use either of these names, Zozo or Sayoko. I thought they were stupid. Subaru was such a fool, with her soft hair and the way she loved to wander.

Some time after what had happened, I got a phone call from Subaru, and I headed out to meet her, on a bench at a station that she had designated. At that station, she said, there was a vending machine across from the bench all the way at the end, and I was to buy a coffee and wait there. These were Subaru's instructions.

So I bought the coffee and was waiting, as directed, when Subaru came running down the platform. I had wondered what kind of expression she would have on her face, but she looked the same as usual. She snatched the coffee from my hand, pulled open the tab and took a sip.

'Why'd you get black coffee?' Subaru complained immediately. 'So bitter.'

'I didn't expect you'd be the one drinking it,' I said.

Subaru furrowed her brow. 'Haven't you thought about making amends for what you did, Tama?'

'Sorry,' I said quietly.

'You should be really sorry,' Subaru said.

And then we sat there on the bench, chatting for a while.

'Are you still working at Shima?'

'Yeah.'

'Nishino really misses you.'

'He called me, at Shima.'

'The fridge is doing well.'

'Take good care of Zozo.'

'I will.'

'I'll leave the key in the letterbox.'

'Okay.'

'On the phone, Nishino asked me to marry him.'

'Huh?'

'I mean, what could grown-ups be thinking?' Subaru laughed.

'Like I could ever get married,' Subaru said, and then she stood up all of a sudden. 'The least Nishino could have done was put on some underwear. He looked like kind of a pathetic idiot, standing there naked,' Subaru mumbled. And then she uttered a final 'Nishinooo', before taking off, briskly walking back up the platform.

I watched Subaru's departing figure the whole time. That was the last time I saw her.


'She said she was going to Osaka Tower,' Mr Shima told me. According to him, she said she was going to Osaka

Tower, and asked him to lend her some money. And that was it.

I had gone to Shima with Nishino. I had previously told Nishino that I had no interest in going there, but he had begged and pleaded with me, until I reluctantly gave in. Mr Shima stood behind the counter, idly chatting with us as he sautéed garlic.

'How much did Subaru borrow from you? I'll pay you back,' Nishino blurted out.

'Why would you be the one to pay?' Mr Shima asked incredulously, while he garnished a filet of fried horse mackerel with the garlic and some dill.

'I bear responsibility for it,' Nishino said staunchly.

'Subaru didn't say anything about that,' Mr Shima said, setting before us the dish he called 'Spanish-style mackerel'.

I could see Subaru's gloves on a far shelf behind the counter.

'She'll be back here any day now. Once she sees Osaka Tower, she'll feel better,' Mr Shima said. He started washing dishes. He was humming some kind of tune.

Nishino and I ate the Spanish-style mackerel, along with 'Spanish escargot' and sautéed mushrooms, and we each drank a glass of red wine from Spain that had a bull on the label, which Mr Shima had recommended.

'The sautéed mushrooms were Subaru's favourite,' I said quietly, and Nishino nodded.

'I don't know why I didn't treat her to sautéed mushrooms as often as she liked,' he sighed.

When we went outside, there were snow flurries in the air.

'There's a statue of Billiken at Osaka Tower,' Nishino said. 'If you rub the soles of his feet, all your wishes will come true.' Nishino faced forward as he spoke.

'Billiken – you mean the guy with the pointy head?' I asked.

'That's right. I think Subaru will like him,' Nishino replied leisurely.

*I wish I could touch Subaru's hair again*, I thought to myself. Nishino was still facing straight ahead. My next thought was, *I doubt I'll ever see Nishino again*. And then I tried to imagine what Osaka Tower looked like. I had never seen it before. I tried to picture a bright, bustling tower, all lit up. And there at the top was Subaru, smiling.

I stood on tiptoe and kissed Nishino on the cheek. The light snow was starting to cover the hoods of the cars. Subaru and I never did get to make a snowman, after all. I reached out to gently touch the snow on a car hood.

# Keenly

I was Maow's 'lover'. Nishino was her 'good friend'.

Nishino and I used to quarrel and laugh about the different words we used. But it made sense.

Maow is a tortoiseshell cat. Slender, supple and serene. She showed up on my veranda one summer day.

I was fanning myself as I listened to the radio. It was tuned to FEN, the American military station, at a low volume. A song that had been popular about twenty years earlier – when I myself had been twenty years old – was playing. I sang along with it, swaying the fan in time with the music.

I thought I saw something out of the corner of my eye. Without moving, I looked through the screen door and there was a cat. She ambled in circles on the veranda, and then perched on the washing machine. As I watched her, the cat returned my stare.

I put down the fan and called out, 'Meow.' The cat was silent. I tried again, 'Meow,' and the cat gave a mew. It sounded more like 'Maow'.

I opened the screen door. The cat just looked straight up at me, without running away. 'Are you hungry?' I asked. The cat gave another 'Maow'. I went back into the apartment, brought out a plate that had a peach stone left on it and set it on the floor. The cat leapt down softly from the washing machine and began to lick the remaining flesh from the stone. The way that her little tongue darted over the peach stone was lovely to watch. The stone had seemed so small on the plate, but it looked much larger now, when compared to the cat's face above it.

After a while, the cat jumped back onto the washing machine and hopped to the railing of the veranda. Then she vaulted to the ground. The moment she landed, there was a soft sound, like a drop of water.

'Meow,' I called out. The cat turned around.

'Maow,' she replied, and then she was gone.

Ants had started to assemble on the plate that was still out on the veranda. I took a tissue and carefully wrapped up the peach stone in it. I brought it inside and threw the entire tissue package into the rubbish bin.

'I'm going to call you Maow, okay?' I said in a low voice to the cat that was now gone. On the radio, the news was being read in fast-paced English. The clamour of the cicadas echoed in the trees of the park before me.

'Maow.' I tried saying it in a slightly louder voice. It had a nice ring to it.

'Maow,' I called out once more. And then I headed towards the bathroom to take a shower.

*

It was around that same time – when Maow started showing up at my apartment – that Nishino and I had our first conversation. Nishino lived in the apartment next door to mine. Both of us had moved in when the building had been completed, so we had been neighbours for at least five years. But it was only after Maow had started coming by that we began having frequent conversations. Up until then, even if we passed in the corridor, we would only nod at each other while trying to avoid eye contact.

Nishino's voice called out just as I was getting some horse mackerel ready for Maow on the veranda.

There was a heavy brown plate that I had decided to use for putting food out for her. Some time before, I had bought it on a whim at a small antique shop located along the route from my building to the station. The shop was crammed with bowls and teacups and saké cups. The design of the plate featured two or three carp swimming around the edge. It may have been an antique but, perhaps because it was chipped, it hadn't been all that expensive. I had washed it well (the shop was a bit dusty inside) and had been putting it out with things like dried sardines on it.

'That's a nice plate,' Nishino said, looking up at me where I stood on the veranda, which was slightly elevated from the ground.

'Yes,' I replied. I must have worn a sceptical look.

'Is that for the cat?' Nishino went on, seeming not to have noticed my expression.

'It is.' I thought about saying, It's for Maow, not just any cat. But the desire not to offer up Maow's name so easily won out.

Nishino didn't move; he just stood there looking up. I set down the plate I was holding on the floor of the veranda. Nishino's upturned face bore a slight resemblance to Maow's. There was something feral, and yet delicate, in his expression. Though he must have been well past thirty, there was still a strange youthfulness about him.

Soon enough, Maow arrived, mewing true to her name. She ate the boiled horse mackerel heartily. As I watched Maow, I completely forgot about Nishino. Once Maow had polished off the fish, she jumped onto the railing and plopped down onto the street.

'Meow,' Nishino called out. Maow had nestled up to him. She allowed herself to be petted by him, closing her eyes halfway and purring.

'She's a friendly cat,' Nishino said as he petted Maow.

'She really is,' I replied, feigning calm, but on the inside I was annoyed. Why should she purr for a random guy like him?

'Maybe I'll try feeding her too,' Nishino said, with the same amiability as Maow.

I just smiled weakly, without replying. Then I picked up the plate and hurried into my apartment. Nishino had been looking up as if he was about to say something else, but I smacked the glass door closed.

'I thought you were kind of scary,' Nishino later reminisced to me. At the time, my mood had been rather scary. I had no way of knowing that, two months later, I would become something like a lover to Nishino.

\*

Nishino slipped into my apartment the same way that Maow slipped onto my veranda.

He may not have cried out, 'Maow,' but Nishino stole into my heart just as smoothly as she did. I only had to leave the door ajar and beckon him inside – first with peanuts or crackers instead of a peach stone – and in good time he too was welcomed with his own plate and bowl.

'Does the cat come every day?' Nishino asked.

'She's not "the cat", she's Maow,' I corrected him, which made Nishino laugh.

'I've been calling him Prince Meow.'

'Well, it's a she, and Maow suits her better anyway.' As I said this, Nishino planted a light kiss on me. Then he picked up Maow's heavy plate, which was under the low table.

'This is a nice piece of pottery,' Nishino said, scrutinizing the plate.

'It was cheap.'

'It's a waste to use it for Maow.'

'Maow's my lover, after all.'

'Maow's your lover, is she?' Nishino laughed. 'So then, what does that make me, Eriko?'

'My good friend, I suppose.'

Nishino laughed, and he kissed me, this time more deeply than before.

'Is this what good friends do?' Nishino asked, his voice soft.

'Of course,' I replied, grinning.

'Maow really is your number one,' Nishino said, as if he was very unhappy about it. Although his eyes were beaming.

'Maow is tops for me, and I'm tops for her.'

'Well, I guess that means I'm just a good friend – not only for you, Eriko, but for Maow too.'

Nishino heaved an exaggerated sigh. Then he covered his face with his hands and pretended to start sobbing.

'Oh, don't be so disheartened,' I said. Nishino peered out from between his fingers, and in the next instant, he let out a huge laugh. I laughed in unison with him.

'You're really cool, Eriko,' Nishino said in a falsetto, embracing me. Then he lay my body down gently on the rug, and kissed me ever so tenderly.

Maow's brown plate was above my head, and every so often my outstretched arm would touch it, making a clattering sound. I had started to fall in love with Nishino. At any moment, I was about to fall in love with him. But I wouldn't love Nishino. I absolutely refused to love him. I had already decided that.

I had failed at marriage once already. My husband and I had been deeply in love with each other. But things fell apart. It wasn't my husband's fault; it wasn't my fault either. We just knew that it didn't work. One day. Out of the blue.

It's not that I've lost my nerve. But since then, perhaps, I'm much more watchful, much more pensive. And when it comes to love, watchfulness and pensiveness lead to a sense of hesitation.

'Why can't I be your lover, Eriko?' Nishino asked me this constantly. Like a spoiled child. A thirty-five-year-old brat. One who was five years younger than me, at that.

'Because I can't be responsible for you,' I replied, caressing Nishino's cheek.

'I don't know why you say such arrogant things to me,' Nishino said, with indignance.

'Arrogant?'

'It's arrogant to think that you can take responsibility for another person. It's patronizing.'

'I see your point.' I nodded. As I continued to nod, Nishino grew more indignant.

'I'm not looking for your admiration – I want you to be my lover!' There was outrage in Nishino's tone but, again, his eyes were beaming.

If Nishino felt some kind of attachment to me, it was probably because I treated him coolly. The moment I stopped being cool towards him, I had no doubt that Nishino would bolt. I would have done the same. Nishino and I were of a similar ilk. That was my conclusion, after much watchfulness and pensive consideration.

'There is something very sincere about Maow,' I said, and Nishino hung his head in disappointment.

'You mean you trust a random cat more than you trust me?'

'Well, I guess that's what it comes down to.'

'Do you really think so little of me?'

Nishino seemed like the epitome of a frivolous man. After ten o'clock at night, Nishino's mobile phone rang again and again. It was always a woman calling. And Nishino was amiable and kind to each one of them. When Nishino came to my place, I would ask him to turn off his phone. His response was always the same.

'I will, as soon as you let me be your lover.'

'There's something wrong with you, Nishino,' I said.

Nishino nodded, a grave look on his face. 'I know better than anyone that there's something wrong with me.'

Although Nishino always had a certain derisiveness about him, when he said this, he seemed deadly serious.

'Okay, then, from now on, you ought to walk the straight and narrow path,' I said.

Nishino looked up at me and sighed.

'I'm scared to even take the first step.'

'What are you scared of?'

'You know, that I'll end up with a straight and narrow life.'

'And you would hate that?'

'It's not that I would hate it – it's that I'm scared of it.'

Nishino uttered these words quickly. Then he buried his face in my chest and was still for a few moments.

'I love women's breasts,' Nishino liked to say. His mobile phone rang, but Nishino didn't answer it.

'Shouldn't you get that?' I asked.

'No. I don't want to,' Nishino replied. 'I'm serious, you know.'

He went on, 'You're being mean, Eriko.' His head was still buried in my breasts. I was idly staring at Maow's plate. I was on the verge of falling in love with Nishino but, I told myself, I couldn't love him. I thought about how strange the word 'love' was. It was just like the inside of the antique shop where I had bought Maow's plate. Totally silent, and dusty. Mementos from long ago piled up in a jumble. Sort of nostalgic, and sad.

Still buried in my chest, Nishino was quiet, his eyes closed.

Nishino left just before Maow left.

'I'm being transferred,' Nishino said.

'Oh?' I replied. My voice was calm.

'Eriko, why don't you marry me?' As Nishino said this, he shifted his body aslant, so as to avoid my gaze.

I giggled. But other than that I didn't reply.

Nishino glanced at me, but quickly averted his eyes. Maow had left bits of grilled sardine on her plate. Instead of looking at me, Nishino stared at the sardines.

'Would you like some sardines?' I asked.

'I would,' Nishino replied in a low voice. 'I wish I were Maow. Then you would give me sardines or mackerel every day.'

The tone of his voice was facetious, so I laughed. But in the next moment, my laughter stopped when I noticed that Nishino's eyes weren't beaming this time.

'Are you actually being serious?' I asked.

Nishino lowered his gaze. 'I'm not sure myself,' he replied. 'All this time, I've been careful not to end up that way.'

I had to laugh at what he'd said about being 'careful'. And now Nishino laughed with me. It would soon be time for me to extricate myself from Nishino. My instincts warned me not to get too close to him. Otherwise, I really would fall for him. And Nishino might even end up falling in love with me too.

Quietly, I carried Maow's plate to the sink. I scraped the

sardine bits into the strainer and started washing the plate. I could feel Nishino's eyes on me. Almost painfully, I felt his gaze settle on my shoulders as I stood before the sink.

*My only lover is Maow, only Maow.* I recited this, like a mantra, as I ran the water.

'Eriko.' Nishino said my name.

'What?' I replied lightly, my back still facing Nishino.

'Eriko,' Nishino repeated. I still didn't turn around. Maow's plate was so clean it glistened, but I kept on rinsing it.

'I'll call you,' Nishino said. 'I'll call every night.'

'Good,' I replied, still with my back to him.


Then Nishino was gone.

Even after he had left my apartment, I kept washing Maow's plate. The plate gleamed. Usually it looked old and kind of weathered, but under the water it had a pretty sparkle.

*I made it through*, I thought to myself. I managed to get through this quite well. Without ever falling in love. And by not falling in love, I didn't inflict any harm. I didn't sustain any harm either.

I took a leisurely bath, even put on a mask and gave myself a manicure. I kept checking in with myself, testing whether or not my heart was churning, but whatever waves I felt were only ripples.

I got into bed, closed my eyes and tried to fall asleep. But sleep proved rather elusive. I thought about Maow. Tomorrow I would treat Maow to some tuna sashimi.

The moment I decided this, though, the waves rolled in. Big, roiling swells. I missed Nishino. I wasn't in love with him, I tried to tell myself through clenched teeth. It wasn't love. I just – I shouldn't have allowed myself to get this close to him. I repeated this to myself.

Sleep finally began to descend upon me. But then it occurred to me that Nishino's mobile phone hadn't rung that night. There hadn't been a single interruption from the girls who were always calling him.

I realized, just before drifting off, that Nishino must have turned his phone off. And as soon as I realized this, I fell into a deep sleep. A part of me feared that Nishino may have actually meant what he'd said.


I tried to recall when it was that Maow left.

The last time I saw Maow was New Year's Eve – I'm sure of that. She had polished off the salmon that was left over from the *kombu-maki* rolls I had made. When I called out to her, 'Maow,' she had replied in turn, 'Maow.' As usual.

But from the next day on, Maow stopped showing up. I had a good laugh, thinking to myself that she must have taken a holiday because of the New Year, but a week went by, and then a month, and still no sign of Maow.

It had been three months since Nishino left, and his calls were becoming less frequent.

'I've been abandoned, by my lover and by my good friend.' I'd murmur these words to myself sometimes, as I stepped out onto the veranda in the winter sunshine. I missed Maow. I tried saying it out loud. 'I miss you, Maow.' I didn't say a word about missing Nishino. Naturally.

I washed Maow's plate well and put it away on a low shelf

in the cupboard. Cats other than Maow sometimes appeared on my veranda, but I didn't feed them. Every so often, I would vividly recall Nishino's voice and expressions, the way he could be both aloof and sensitive at the same time.

What was it that Nishino was afraid of? And what about me – why had I been afraid to love Nishino? At the time, it had all seemed perfectly clear to me, but now, in hindsight, everything was vague. Maow's lithe movements were no longer distinct in my memory either.

I wondered if, even now, in whatever faraway place Nishino was, he was being careful not to fall in love with someone. Was he chatting up all the girls – and seducing some of them – in that affable voice of his?

I should have given out sardines and mackerel every day. To Nishino, I mean. Then we might have lived together happily ever after. There are moments when I feel that way. But those moments quickly pass. And then I simply miss Maow. I miss her keenly. 'Maow,' I call out for her. And then, in a quiet voice, I call out his name too.

'Nishino.'

The winter sun continues to shine on the veranda.

# Marimo

It was at the 'Energy-Saving Cooking Club' that I became acquainted with Nishino. The club met twice a month at the home of Mrs Yamamoto, who lived in the neighbourhood. As the name suggested, it was a cooking course for those looking to conserve energy.

It was the slogan I saw on the advertisement in the residential newsletter that motivated me to attend the course. 'The Energy-Saving Cooking Club – economize, reduce waste, and have fun cooking on ¥30,000 a month!'

'This looks promising,' I murmured to myself, having spent the entire morning weeding the garden. I loved the word 'economize' – though I doubted that I was alone in that regard, amongst other full-time housewives.

'Economize'. 'Worth the price'. 'Bargain'. I was enchanted by such words and phrases. During the so-called 'high-speed growth' period and what was referred to as the 'bubble years', and even throughout the recession that followed – I had come to love hearing these words, no matter what era we were in. That's not to say that I don't spend money. I have a thirty-year mortgage on a two-storey, ready-built, thirteen-hundred-square-foot house with an attached garage and a nine-hundred-square-foot garden. I sent my two daughters to university. And I gave those girls a proper wedding reception, with a seating chart and everything. My family's ancestral burial plot requires a plane trip to get to it, so I entombed some of the ashes in a new grave at a massive cemetery an hour's drive away. This enables us to get to the grave easily (visiting graves being a hobby of my husband's for the last few years although, until my daughters grew up, his hobbies had involved more active outdoor activities), and my husband traded in the white Nissan Sunny that we had had for twenty-three years for a red Nissan March. (I personally have no interest in riding around in a red car, but my husband simply insisted. After more than thirty years of living together, I never would have expected that my husband had been yearning for a red car. Life can be so unpredictable, at least when it comes to the colour of car that my husband likes . . . to say nothing about what happened with Nishino.)

After I had finished weeding and was leaning up against the gate, surveying the garden with a feeling of deep self-satisfaction, Mrs Kobayashi, my neighbour from three houses over, called out to me. Whenever I'm gardening, without fail Mrs Kobayashi will pass by and say, 'Ah, Mrs Sasaki, always working so hard!' She patrolled the neighbourhood several times a day, always calling out to each person she came across. My garden must have been included on her 'route', as it were.

'Ah, Mrs Sasaki, always working so hard!'

On that day, Mrs Kobayashi made her stock comment.

If I ran into her at the gate as I was on my way out, it would be, 'And where are you off to?' Or if I were coming home, it was, 'And where have you been?' The pattern was so regular, it was like a tea ceremony.

'It's such a puny little garden, the least I can do is keep the weeds out.'

I had my own pattern of responses. Mrs Kobayashi had a set of topics – the young single people who didn't follow the rules for putting out the rubbish, the declining birth rate, global warming – and she would chatter away about these, without pause, for exactly seven minutes and thirty seconds. I had recently begun timing her, to see just how long she could go on chatting by herself. The longest was thirteen minutes and twenty-five seconds, while the shortest was forty seconds. The brevity of the latter was due to the fact that she was interrupted by a sudden evening rain shower. It seems all humans are fallible in the face of nature's greatness.

Mrs Kobayashi's latest concerns were men and women over the age of thirty who were not married, couples who were married but who weren't having children, and then general ecological awareness, it seemed. Unmarried people and childless couples were the objects of her criticism. Ecology, on the other hand, was the target of her praise, while those who were not ecologically aware naturally became the object of her reproach. Mrs Kobayashi was clearly a dualistic thinker. I would bet she had dabbled in Cartesian theory in her youth.

'The rubbish attracts the crows and we can't have that, can we?' I was able to break in after a moment of silence just past the seven-and-a-half-minute mark. One thing I had learned over the course of twenty-five years living here was that disregarding the etiquette of conversational interjections was a sure-fire way to arouse Mrs Kobayashi's ire. Such as not responding to queries. No matter how vastly imbalanced the exchanges may have been. Needless to say, interpersonal relationships are not mathematically divisible.

However, on that day, Mrs Kobayashi brought news about Mrs Yamamoto's energy-saving cooking club. Without expressing any of her opinions regarding one's freedom not to marry or not to have children, fortunately. Mrs Kobayashi informed me that there was still space available in the club. I decided on the spot to put in a request to join – Mrs Kobayashi served as the membership coordinator.

Nishino stood out among the 'young' ladies who made up the majority of the club's members. (This was how I referred to women of my own generation. The word I liked to use for 'young' was *myorei*, in which the character for *myo* included the pictographs for both 'little' and 'woman', which meant that it was usually used to describe girls as well as young women. However, this same *myo* has several connotations: highly skilled, or unusual, or esoteric. Following this logic – as it occurred to me one day – when *myo* refers to age, its various meanings are more applicable to women 'of a certain age' rather than simply young women.)

For one thing, Nishino was quite a handsome man. Secondly, he was clean-cut. Furthermore, Nishino was kind and courteous. And to top it all off, he had a steady job with a respectable company.

All of this sent the 'young' ladies into a tizzy. I of course was no exception. How can I put it? Yes, that's right – as far as we ladies were concerned, by embodying all these things, Nishino seemed to exemplify the idea of a 'bargain' with his very existence.

'And what is it you do –' Mrs Kobayashi had asked straightaway, after Nishino's background check had passed through the initial stage (during the first break in our cooking practice, the 'young' ladies had casually, and then more openly, flung assorted questions at Nishino like arrows) '– that enables you to slip out of the office? In the middle of the day like this?'

Even to such an obviously rude question, Nishino responded courteously. At the firm where he worked, his department was now involved in the distribution of pots and pans made in Europe. Nowadays, amid demands for ecological awareness, there was a need for cookware that avoided the waste and disposal of ingredients. To this end, he had been dispatched to cooking sites in the field for the purpose of conducting research.

At first, Mrs Kobayashi had listened sceptically to Nishino's formal explanation (he later confided to me that he had assumed that very tone for her benefit – it was one of his sales techniques, he had laughed refreshingly), but her expression had instantly softened at the mention of 'ecology' and 'avoiding waste'. Mrs Kobayashi had been a fan of Nishino's ever since. But having her as a fan meant that, every time, Nishino now found himself subject to Mrs Kobayashi's ritual of perpetual chatter, to which he submitted without complaint. It has long been my opinion that the inattentive cannot keep company with housewives but, even for a company man, he demonstrated considerable skill.

Nishino was not inattentive. Far from it. By his third time attending the energy-saving cooking club, he had won over all of the 'young' ladies. When Nishino entered the classroom, a number of them would rush over and crowd around him. Even the ones who didn't run over would watch out of the corner of their eyes, and whenever Nishino broke into a smile, they would return his smile threefold (the ladies' smiling faces being both literally and figuratively large).

*This could be dangerous*, I thought to myself at first. The sight of a single male seal holding sway over so many female seals – it wasn't pretty, was it? But little by little I too became convinced. The female seals throng around the male seal because they desire him. They aren't submitting themselves to him – clearly they do it joyfully. Perhaps the male seal finds himself at a loss, there among the females. But a male seal couldn't tear himself away from the females, not once they have gathered momentum. Not even our male seal.

I was having more and more fun. Women are beautiful when they are dedicating themselves to something. Or so the magazines often tell us. The 'young' ladies who were dedicated to Nishino were certainly beautiful. Even Mrs Kobayashi ceased her criticism of young and unmarried men and women past the age of thirty. Because Nishino was thirty-seven years old. And a bachelor. Who lived alone in Tokyo. An alluring company man. Yukihiko Nishino.


'Hey, Sayuri Sasaki!' This was what Nishino said, the first time he spoke to me. I was at an art-house cinema, and after the showing had ended and the lights had come up, there – sitting in the seat beside me – was Nishino.

Still suffused with euphoria from the film, I stared at Nishino vacantly. I was surprised that he knew my first name. But I concealed my pleasure, assuming the decorum of a worldly 'young' lady.

'Nishino, what are you doing in a place like this? What about work?' I quickly asked, despite the fact that I had criticized Mrs Kobayashi for being similarly rude.

Nishino hesitated for a moment, and then eventually blurted out, 'I'm playing truant.'

Nishino did not speak to me in the explanatory tone he used with the women at the energy-saving cooking club. Afterwards, while we drank coffee in a café, Nishino told me, 'It's because you seem different from the other ladies, Sayuri.'

The phrase 'you seem different from the others' is generally thought of as a clincher. It's written in all the books. I had always assumed that I would never fall for such a line. But since no one had ever spoken such words to me, I had been unable to confirm whether I could actually remain unfazed when I heard them.

*All is lost*, I thought to myself at the time. The moment he said those words to me, I forgave Nishino everything. Even though, up until that point, there wasn't a single thing that Nishino needed me to forgive him for.

I forgave Nishino his past, I forgave Nishino his present and I forgave Nishino his eternal future.

While we drank coffee, Nishino and I discussed the film we had just seen. Then we talked about the cooking club and, finally, we touched upon some of our favourite authors. Among the authors Nishino liked, there was one whom I also liked and one whom I hated. By the time we had finished drinking our coffee, I no longer disliked that author all that much. Nishino called me by my name several times. Sayuri.

'Do you always address women that way, by their first names?' I asked.

'About half the time, I guess,' Nishino replied. His words cut through me. Of course I hadn't expected him to say, 'Only with you, Sayuri.' But I had hoped the answer might be something more along the lines of, 'Almost never.' I was surprised by the way this wounded me.

The afternoon was full of surprises. I was surprised that men like Nishino existed in this world, the type of man who could slip so smoothly into a woman's sensibility. I was surprised by the way, before even being aware of it, I was trying to act out the role of the 'alluring older woman'. I was surprised by how easily emotions such as jealousy or possessiveness could be aroused with regard to a person for whom I harboured not even the slightest feelings.

Not even the slightest feelings? Were my feelings for Nishino actually so slight, after all? Even now, I cannot say. And at the time, I was even less sure.

At some point, Nishino and I found ourselves talking on the phone.

Come to think of it, almost all of my interactions with him were over the telephone. In the morning, after I'd done all of the cleaning and laundry and the house felt as if it were bathed in white. When I was preparing dinner, and the haze inside my head would grow just a bit denser. When I woke up in the middle of the night to go to the bathroom and couldn't fall back asleep, so would sit on the sofa in the living room and just stare off into space. These were the times when Nishino would call me on the phone, as if he were peeking in at me through a hole that had opened up in the wall. This part was crucial. Ultimately, as far as I was concerned, the manner in which Nishino telephoned me was the thing that set him apart as unique.

Surely Nishino must have developed a sixth sense. Without exception, Nishino never called when my husband was by my side, or when one of my daughters had brought my grandchildren over to play. It must have been because I didn't want it that way. On the other hand, had I preferred to sneak in a conversation with Nishino while I was next to my husband, then that would probably have been when Nishino called.

A man who could satisfy a woman's desires that even she was unaware of, who could draw them out from deep within her heart – that was Nishino. None of which seemed very significant. Calling on the phone at the desired time. Calling at the desired frequency. Using the desired words of praise. Offering the desired kindness. Scolding in the desired way. Things so insignificant that no man could pull them off. But Nishino did all of these things with ease. He was detestable – both to men and women.

That's right. People who are too good to be true arouse a certain hatred. Nishino often talked about 'the girl' he was 'seeing now'. Where they had gone on a date. What they had eaten. How they had hit on him (like moths to a flame, the girls always hit on Nishino – without him even realizing that he was being hit on). What kind of sex they had had. What they had accused him of. And finally, how the relationship had gone wrong.

In due course, the girls would accuse him of things, and start to make demands. 'You're too cold' or 'Your head is always in the clouds' or 'You don't love me enough.' These were the kinds of things the girls always complained about. To my mind, in the hearts of these girls, some part of them hated Nishino's perfection. His slippery, elusive perfection.

'You don't cast off your coolness in order to love someone?' I once asked Nishino.

'Sayuri, have you ever loved someone that way?' Nishino tossed the question back at me. His voice was low. It made me shiver. This almost never happened when I was on the phone with Nishino, but I often felt a shiver go through me right before he called me. Could that have been Nishino's intuition running high? During that time, my own intuition was unusually keen.

'I have,' I replied, after giving it some thought. Who was I thinking of at the time? I tried vaguely to call up the face of someone. But a clear image hadn't formed.

*Who did I mean?* I wondered, doubting myself. The memory must have been there. It remained unfocused, but I knew it was there. Could I say that it wasn't Nishino? Perhaps it was. Perhaps it wasn't. Of that, no one – not even myself – could be sure.

\*

At some point, the telephone calls from Nishino stopped abruptly.

During the time I was talking to Nishino, I had not abandoned my mentality towards economizing, price-worthiness and bargains. Humans in general – and housewives in particular – are abundantly able to compartmentalize between this and that. I carried on in the performance of rituals with Mrs Kobayashi, and I did not neglect the weeding of the garden. I even boasted perfect attendance at the energy-saving cooking club. I had been steadily making *kinpira* from daikon peelings and Chinese stir-fry from the outer leaves of cabbage, serving these at my table as well as faxing the recipes to both of my daughters. Though I didn't know whether or not they had made any of the recipes themselves.

I realized there hadn't been any calls from Nishino a week after he stopped phoning me. In truth, my body knew sooner than that, but my mind refused to admit it. Nishino was also absent from the cooking club (Nishino had perfect attendance, like me, a fact in which I took untold secret pleasure), and each of the club members were saddened by this.

It was at the next meeting that we all found out that Nishino had left the club. I too heard it for the first time then.

I tried to remember what Nishino had talked about the last time we spoke. Trifling things. The dog he had had a long time ago. The scent of the perfume that the girl he was seeing now used. What kind of sound did the ocean make at night? Those were the kinds of things that Nishino had mentioned. It was always like that. Not once did he ever bring up anything of consequence. Then again, there aren't many things in this world that are really of any consequence. Perhaps there are none at all.

I suffered for three months, thinking about Nishino. Needless to say, during that time I maintained perfect attendance at the cooking club, and I carried on regularly with the weeding, and interacted with the neighbours. But as I went about my life, adhering to my mentality towards economizing, bargains and price-worthiness, I thought constantly of Nishino's sweet, low voice.

As those three painful months were drawing to a close, I found myself standing idly in front of a pet shop in the middle of the shopping district. Not thinking about what kind of dog Nishino used to have. I was just vaguely watching the dogs. 'Young' ladies like me, we tend to think of things in abstraction, much more than most people realize.

Inside the shop, there were tanks of tropical fish and goldfish lined up. My mind still a total blank, I ventured into the store. Then I remembered my older daughter had bought a red-eared slider turtle from this shop. The turtle, which she had named Dolly, had lived a long time. Next to the aquarium of guppies, there was a tank filled with the green moss balls called *marimo*. There were many of them, in all different sizes, sunk on the bottom of the tank. I reached out my hand and touched the surface of the water. The *marimo* – all of them, large and small – were utterly still. *Marimo* are found at the bottom of lakes, where they gradually grow bigger. My younger daughter had written a composition about them when she was in school. Mustn't the *marimo* get lonely? – she had included that line in her essay.

*Mustn't the marimo get lonely?* I repeated these words over and over in my head as I stared at the *marimo*. The *marimo* seemed very much like Nishino. This thought occurred to me, for some reason. For an instant, I considered buying one of the *marimo*, bringing it home and putting it in the sunny spot on top of the sideboard in the living room, as a memento of my feelings for him. But I gave up the idea. 'Young' ladies like me, we have a tendency towards unsentimentality, much more so than most people realize.

As I stared at the *marimo*, I thought about the sound of Nishino's voice. I thought about Nishino's selfishness. I thought about Nishino's tenderness. I thought about all the things I could remember about Nishino. And then, at last, I thought about that moment when I had forgiven him for everything. I reminisced about it all, everything up until the end, to my heart's content.

Once these thoughts stopped running through my head, I knew that my period of suffering was over. I had fond memories of Nishino. That was how I felt. And yet, I knew this was a lie.

I thought back over it. *Why only remember the good parts?*

Ten years from now, if I'm still alive, I'll come back and buy a *marimo*. I'll put it in a glass bowl and set it out in a sunlit spot.

The sun was setting, and the streetlights were starting to go on in the shopping district. Would I still be here in another ten years? Would I still be able to recall Nishino's voice?

'Goodbye, Nishino,' I said softly, and I waved to the

aquarium filled with *marimo*. When I left the shop, all of the other shops were brightly lit up. I was lost among the bustle of the evening street.

# Grapes

Nishino quickly let out a sigh.

'Thirty million years from now, this place will merge with the Andromeda Galaxy,' he said.

'When you say "this place", just which place do you mean?' I asked, and Nishino let out an even deeper sigh.

'I mean the Earth and the Sun and Pluto and even the stars further away – all of it,' he replied.

'So, is there something wrong with this place being joined up with Andromeda?'

'It would be brighter. Meaning, it wouldn't get dark at night.'

When I looked at Nishino's face, his brow was furrowed and his expression was serious.

'I think it would be nice if it didn't get dark at night,' I said softly.

Nishino shook his head. 'A world without darkness is unthinkable.'

Nishino pulled on my hair as he said this. I think he

thought of this as a demonstration of affection. I, however, did not appreciate having my hair pulled.

'Andromeda contains so many stars, there's no way it would ever be night,' Nishino explained. 'It would always be daytime. Everything filled with light. There would be no shadows.' Nishino gave another sigh.

'Does that mean that there wouldn't be any more cloudy days either?' I asked.

'Well, there would probably still be clouds.'

'What about rainy days?'

'It would probably still rain.'

'That would be okay, then,' I said. I liked rainy days. And I liked cloudy days even more. The day when I had first met Nishino had been a blazing sunny day.

It was at the end of the summer, in Enoshima. My relatives ran a beachside refreshment shack, and I worked there part-time. Every weekend, both Saturday and Sunday, I worked two days straight. From the beginning of July, when the beach shack opened, to early September, when they closed it up, I commuted down to Enoshima, never missing a day. I may have been feeling a bit bored and adrift – since, although I had been accepted at my first-choice university, soon after classes had started the previous spring I began to find them dull and so rarely showed my face on campus – nevertheless I had always loved the beach shack. I had been working there every year since middle school.

Nishino had been accompanied by a woman. She looked to be just past thirty, with short hair and a very nice figure. Nishino was in his mid-fifties, which meant that she was quite a bit younger, but Nishino was youthful – in appearance as well as in substance – so the age difference between them didn't seem so vast.

No matter how chic or urbane the men and women might have appeared when they arrived in Enoshima in their street clothes, once they had changed into bathing suits and were eating sea snails cooked in their own shells and buying nacre key rings in the souvenir shops, they were no different from other 'native Japanese'. Enoshima was the kind of place that had an equalizing effect.

However, the woman who had accompanied Nishino was different. She wore a gold chain around her slender ankle. Her pedicure was the colour of the deep ocean. She may have looked like a Japanese person, but her mien called to mind a place far from Enoshima. Perhaps the deserted beach of an unknown southern island. Or the white sands of a dark and looming seaside forest.

'That girl – it was like she was always off in the clouds. She didn't seem to belong anywhere.' This had been Nishino's reply some time later, when I had remarked on my impression of the woman who had been with him.

'Why would you break up with such a charming lady?' I asked.

Nishino stifled a laugh. 'Because, I fell in love with you, Ai!'

'So, Nishino, you mean to say that, when you fall for the next girl, you break up with the previous girl right away?' I asked, raising my voice. Nishino opened his eyes wide and peered closely at my face. His look seemed to say, You're so young, yet you're so quaintly old-fashioned.

'I do not break up with them right away,' Nishino replied, after a moment had passed.

'Which means you two-time?'

'I would if I could, but usually the girl doesn't stand for it.'

'So then, what happens?'

'I end up getting dumped. By both of them.'

Once it comes out – in some way or another – that he's been two-timing, things are a mess for a couple of weeks. About a month later, the strong-willed ones (and occasionally a weak-willed one) will make up her mind to leave. As for the girl who's left behind, the situation with her remains cheerful and pleasant for an average of three months. But once the thrill of victory is gone, the girl begins to reflect calmly upon Nishino's past behaviour and, by the fourth month, the accusations begin to fly that Nishino is two-timing again. And then it's not just about two-timing – the fifth month brings full-scale complaints that Nishino is constitutionally commitment-phobic or that he has a deep-rooted tendency for cheating. I just can't trust you any more, and so on. I still love you, but it's too painful. These were the kinds of things said by the girl who's left behind when, ultimately, in the sixth month, she leaves.

'It takes about half a year to reach this "final conclusion",' Nishino said with a laugh. 'It's like the laws of physics. Why is it that, eventually, all girls end up adhering to the same formula in their response, no matter whether they are chubby or skinny, laid-back or uptight, conventionally beautiful or idiosyncratically striking, pescatarians or red-blooded meat-lovers?' Nishino inclined his head in wonder.

I myself was just as baffled by Nishino, a man in his mid-fifties who resembled boys my own age, teenagers who thought of nothing but girls.

'Nishino, do you really believe that all girls are exactly the same?' I asked.

'I could be wrong,' Nishino said leisurely. 'All the girls I've ever known, at least, they've all been the same, down to the last.'

*Well, then, the girls you date must all be pretty boring,* I thought fleetingly, but I immediately regretted feeling mean towards all the girls Nishino had dated whom I had never laid eyes on. I bet one would be hard-pressed to find a girl out there who qualified as 'boring'. More likely, they were quite a bit scarcer than boys who were 'boring'. I would have said as much to Nishino, but I figured he would make fun of me or call me a nit-picker, saying I must be in favour of female supremacy, so I kept my mouth shut.

'Are you angry?' Nishino asked. I had grown very quiet and still. 'I don't mean you, Ai. I'm sure you're different,' Nishino went on.

*'Not you, you're different'* – *that was pretty clichéd, wasn't it?* I thought to myself. This guy Nishino was like some kind of sweetheart swindler.

'I mean it, Ai. There's something about you that's different from all the other girls I've ever known.' Nishino grinned, and then he kissed me. I kept my eyes open and stayed still.

No doubt the thing about me that differed from all the other girls was that I didn't harbour the smallest bit of yearning for Nishino. It wasn't just Nishino, for that matter – I had never harboured feelings for a boy at all, not once. Sure, I liked going out drinking or seeing a movie or simply talking with them just fine, but I had never really fallen for one or found any of them particularly memorable. Not in all of my eighteen years.

So. I had met Nishino at the beachside shack. He had been accompanied by the short-haired woman with the nice figure. The following week, Nishino came back again. This time, he was by himself.

'Are there any good bars around here?' Nishino had first said to me. *This old guy seems out of place,* I had thought.

'There are, if you don't mind walking a bit, in the opposite direction from the station,' I said, giving him an earnest answer anyway.

'What time do you get off?' Nishino persisted.

I was silent. I had no obligation to tell a complete stranger information like that. I had just spun around and was about to retreat inside when, from behind me, I heard him apologize.

'Sorry, that was a rude thing to ask.' Nishino spoke in a soft voice.

Later, I told Nishino that his apology had seemed to reflect the wisdom of age, and he had nodded.

'As I've grown older, I've come to realize – all too well – that things like manners and reason are not simply for appearance's sake. What's more, even when you're as polite as can be, personal relationships can still fall to pieces. People are very complicated, you know.' Nishino sighed as he said this.

I had plenty of doubts about just how polite (principally, to women) and reasonable (again, principally, to women)

Nishino had actually been. He had yet to demonstrate either of these qualities to me, at least. Or so I thought.


'You've got a boyfriend, haven't you?' Kikumi said to me not long after I had met Nishino.

'Not really,' I replied. Kikumi was staring fixedly at the area around the nape of my neck.

'Then how come you're hardly ever at your place lately? How come you get so many phone calls from some guy who just says, "It's me," without giving his name? How come sometimes you smell like a certain unfamiliar cologne, Ai?' Kikumi asked in a single breath.

I told Kikumi I thought she sounded like a girl chiding her boyfriend for having an affair, and she narrowed her eyes at me.

'Who's the guy?' Kikumi asked, peering at my face.

'Nobody, really.'

'What's he like? Does he drive a car? Or a motorcycle?'

'Probably neither.'

'Is he nice?'

'Yeah, I guess.'

'What kind of dates do you usually have?'

'We usually go to his place.'

'Where does this guy live?'

'In Taito-ku.'

'Hmm,' Kikumi murmured. 'He sounds pretty refined. I mean, sounds like he makes a living.' She took a sip of *hojicha* as she said this.

I had met Kikumi at our university's matriculation

ceremony. We were in the same department and had been assigned seats next to each other. Her last name is Kasahara, mine is Kase.

Kikumi hadn't really been going to class either. She commuted from home, though, so she spent a lot of time at my place.

'My parents annoy me whenever I'm home,' she said. 'As long as I pretend to go to class, they rest easy. They have no idea that I'm holing up here.' Kikumi took another sip of *hojicha*.

Kikumi was a lesbian. It hadn't even been six months since she admitted it to herself, which was why she didn't have a proper girlfriend yet. Kikumi had relayed this to me in a detached manner the second time she came over to hang out at my place.

'I thought you might be a lesbian too, Ai. That's why I decided to confide in you,' Kikumi had gone on.

'Nope, not me. I've never been in love with a guy, but I've never been in love with a girl either. I guess you could say that I'm as yet undecided about whether I'm homosexual or heterosexual, but I think I'm probably heterosexual. Even though there's no basis for it.'

I had thought about it carefully as I spoke, and when I was finished, Kikumi had laughed.

'Ai, there's something very rigorous about you. You must be quite the scholar.'

'Sure, I can work and I do like to study. Just once, I got the top grade in every subject – straight fives,' I told Kikumi, and she let out a little whoop.

'That's awesome. Even in gym and music, wow!'

The time I got straight fives had been the first term of my first year in middle school. In music, there had been no practical test and, in gym, we had played ping-pong for the entire term. I'm tone deaf, and I have slow reflexes, but I happen to excel at ping-pong. My relatives who ran the Enoshima beachside shack, their family's main business was a small ryokan, and there was a shabby old ping-pong table at the inn. I had been playing ping-pong against my older cousins since primary school. It goes without saying, though, that I never got straight fives again.

'Anyway, make sure you're straight with this guy,' Kikumi said with a deadpan expression. 'Because, Ai, you make it seem like you're playing it straight, when really your attentions are elsewhere.' Kikumi seemed to be looking right through me, as if to say, 'I'm on to you.'

'I got it. I'll do my best to play it straight,' I promised Kikumi. Meanwhile, I marvelled at how different her impression of 'this guy' and who Nishino actually was must have been.

Nishino was delighted when I told him about this exchange with Kikumi. Even more delighted than I had expected.

'You know, lately, I've been wondering what's going on,' Nishino said.

Nishino and I were in his bed. Apparently, our bodies were well suited to each other. Nishino had been the one to say so, and he was probably right.

'I may have slept with a lot of girls, but you're the best, Ai,' Nishino told me. 'You might think that I use that word a lot – the "best" – but you would be sorely mistaken. To say someone is the best, well, that just ends up reminding a girl about how many other girls I've been with. No – rarely have I dared to utter such a startling admission.' I couldn't tell whether Nishino was being boastful or self-deprecating.

'Hmm,' I murmured in response. I had no idea whether sex with Nishino was good, bad or average. It wasn't that I hadn't had sex before, just that the sample wasn't large enough for me to be able to discern if this sex was good or bad.

'Do you like me, Ai?' Nishino asked, trailing his lips along my throat.

'I like you,' I replied, without skipping a beat. Had I given myself time to think, my mind would have started wandering. I had learned from Nishino that one mustn't be vague – neither in speech nor in conduct – while in the throes of passion.

'You should know, Ai,' Nishino had explained to me at one point, 'when you get to be my age, vigour becomes quite important. Once you lose momentum, well, it's all over. Everything goes to hell, as if you've been swallowed up by a big, gaping crevice that's opened up in the ground. You might never recover.'

At first I had no idea what Nishino was talking about. Like I said, my experience was limited to boys in their teens or early twenties. It was only after this conversation had gone on for quite some time that I finally realized Nishino was referring to erections. This came as a surprise to me, having always assumed that boys would get an erection at any time, that it wasn't a question of 'could' – I had thought they managed to do it even when they weren't in the mood.

'You're so honest, Nishino,' I said, a little impressed.

'It's because honesty, manners and reason are important to me,' he said. This was a mantra of Nishino's. Why Nishino bothered with the likes of me, I'll never know. What was it about me – a not-yet-fully-formed creature – that a grown-up like Nishino found attractive? Maybe it was actually my lack of development that he liked. I once mumbled something to him, along these lines, and Nishino thought about it for a moment before shaking his head.

'Ai, in addition to the fact that you're more mature than any grown woman, you're also purer than any chaste young girl,' he said.

'That's quite an embarrassing way of putting it,' I said with surprise, and Nishino took me in his arms. He held me tightly for a moment.

I always suspected that Nishino saw something beyond me, some other version of the story. The real me was quite different, but his take on things made him feel good.

Nishino would probably insist that he wasn't the kind of guy who harboured illusions. He'd probably also say something like, that was the reason why, after all these years, he had never married – that in the end, he wasn't capable of carrying out a passionate love affair. But the truth was that Nishino *did* seem like the dreamy type who harboured illusions. Not that I had any idea what kinds of dreams those were.

Nishino and I spent the entire afternoon in bed. He had slipped out of the office to come and meet me.

'I can't wait until the evening to see you,' Nishino often said to me lately. 'I miss your face, Ai. I want to feel your breath on my cheek. I want to hear your voice directly in my ear.' Nishino would murmur these things to me.

'I must be out of my mind,' Nishino would go on. 'Do you like me, Ai?' He would ask me the same question as before. And I would reply the same way, on the spot.

'I like you.'

Nishino would furrow his brow. Then, after moving around a bit, he would ejaculate. He was very adept at coming on my stomach.

'Use a condom,' I'd say to him, but Nishino never did.

Instead he would say, 'Never have sex when it's near your ovulation day.' And the truth was, Nishino never tried to have sex around that time.


'That's dangerous,' Kikumi said. She was making a passing comment about Nishino's recent obsession with me. 'He'll get laid off before he knows it, if he keeps playing truant like that.'

'It's a small company, and he's like his own boss, so he won't get laid off,' I replied in an uncertain tone.

Kikumi rolled her eyes. 'Who does this guy think he is?'

Kikumi asked so many questions about Nishino, I ended up having to promise to introduce them to each other. I dreaded it. I imagined that the elusive, ephemeral quality of my relationship with Nishino – which may or may not have been real – would dissipate if it weren't just the two of us alone together.

Our relationship was fleeting. That's what I liked about it. But if the two of us were to spend time with someone else, I dreaded that it might provide external confirmation of the relationship between Nishino and me – validating us as 'a couple'. As soon as that happened, it would be like pinning a bill to the wall, and eventually we would be forced to settle accounts.

On the day I had promised to introduce them, Kikumi showed up wearing ridiculously high heels. In these heels, Kikumi was even taller than Nishino. On her wrists and around her neck and fingers, she was adorned with twice as many accessories as usual. Her make-up was heavier too. I thought she looked like someone who was dressed up for a Shinto festival.

Kikumi peered at Nishino's face with her intense gaze. Nishino returned her look with steady eyes. I sat idly beside them. Quite suddenly, I was struck by a recollection of the angle of Nishino's erection.

We were at a coffee shop that Kikumi had specified. Kikumi had ordered a coffee, decisively, so Nishino and I had followed suit and ordered coffees as well. The coffee was quite delicious. Sunlight poured through the shop's windows. There were two white tulips in a crystal vase on the table.

At first we were quiet. Kikumi ordered another coffee. Nishino and I each ordered another coffee too. Nishino was laughing. His face was deadly serious, but just one layer beneath the skin he was chuckling to himself. I myself felt a little like crying. Kind of like an idiot. Both Kikumi and I had been alive for less than half the time that Nishino had. And besides, I didn't even like Nishino all that much. Or so I thought.

'Are you hungry?' Nishino said after a while. As we had

been sitting in silence, apart from each other, time had passed and, before we knew it, the sun was starting to set.

'I am,' I said quickly. Even though I wasn't really all that hungry.

'I'm not hungry, but I would have a drink,' Kikumi said slowly. Kikumi's lips were very pretty. They were a shiny and glossy pearl pink.

'Nishino, what is it you like about Ai?' Kikumi asked, as if this were part of an ongoing conversation.

'Ah, I too would like to have someone explain that to me,' Nishino replied quietly. As if it were part of an ongoing conversation. 'In all my life, this may well be the most deviant situation I've ever found myself in.' Nishino spoke pretty calmly for a deviant.

Kikumi kept her gaze focused on Nishino. Nishino returned it just as fixedly. One might even have taken the two of them for lovers.

I drank down the last of my coffee. There was only a little bit left in the cup, but I took my time finishing it off. I could hear a buzzing sound over by the counter. It must have been the noise of coffee beans being ground. Just then, I felt a fervent desire to fall in love with Nishino. I wanted to love Nishino in a way that would make him love me. That's what I was thinking. But the fact was that I didn't love him. The electric coffee grinder kept buzzing away in the background.


'Hey, we should die together.'

I can't quite remember the first time that Nishino said

this to me. I think it was around when I was about to start commuting to Enoshima again, so almost a year must have passed since I had met Nishino. Although I had spent little time on campus during the previous year, I hadn't failed any of my courses. That was because, as much as possible, I had tried to enrol in classes where exams and reports mattered more than attendance. I got lots of As because I still happened to like studying. I had turned twenty. And as before, I hardly ever went in to university, seeing Nishino three times a week instead.

'If I keep meeting up with you in the daytime, it stands to reason the company will go under,' Nishino had started saying, so our dates were all day Sunday, and then two other evenings in the middle of the week.

'The boss can't take Saturdays off!' Nishino said this with a note of tedium. 'Had I known, I might never have started my own company. I'd have taken an undemanding position in government service, so that I could spend all my time the way I like – with you, Ai.' Nishino's tone was semi-serious.

'Starting in July, I'll be working in Enoshima, so we won't be able to see each other on Sundays,' I told him.

Nishino went pale. 'I don't like that at all!' he cried. Immediately, he looked embarrassed for having cried out.

'What's become of me?' Nishino would sometimes utter. 'This is why I have never, to this day, loved a woman, in the true sense of the word,' he would continue in a low voice. 'Even though it seems meaningless to say "in the true sense of the word".' Nishino would laugh a little as he said this. I liked the way he looked when he laughed best. His handsome features would give way to a sort of unguardedness.

'We're not going to die together,' I would reply.

'I worry about leaving you behind, Ai.'

'I'm perfectly capable of taking care of my own affairs. And, anyway, it's very strange to talk about who you'll leave behind.'

'I can't stand the thought of you having sex with other men, Ai.'

'But even now, I could do that any time I wanted to.'

My reply had been reflexive, and after it came out, I covered my mouth. What I had said was mean. And I hated meanness. What it did to both the perpetrators and to the victims.

Nishino's expression again looked embarrassed. 'I mean, really, what am I saying? I sound like a young girl,' he said, and let out a sigh.

'Hey, let's have sex right now,' Nishino said. And then, without waiting for my response, he took me roughly.

*I guess I like rough sex*, I thought to myself. It also occurred to me that perhaps I preferred the way that Nishino had sex to Nishino himself. But then again, Nishino's way of having sex was also a part of Nishino himself. I caught myself before I got too deep in thought. Mustn't lose momentum.

Nishino finished, rough and quick. We laid in the bed, stroking each other's bellies. Nishino's stomach was supple. Mine was taut.

'Hey, we should die together.' Nishino said it once more. In a soft voice. I strained my ears to try to determine whether or not there was a note of madness concealed in the softness. Nishino repeated himself, over and over. 'We should die together.'

At the end of August, Kikumi and Nishino came to see me in Enoshima. The day was frenetic from early in the morning. Such a strange word, 'frenetic'. But that's what it was. I murmured it to myself, three times over. 'Frenetic.' Then I said it to Kikumi and Nishino. They laughed as they drank their *amazaké*.

Nishino and Kikumi put up an umbrella on the beach. Nishino spent the whole time sprawled on the sand. Kikumi went into the ocean every so often. And I, as I said, was too frenetic to even take a break and go out to see them.

Once it was evening, when the waves got a little bigger and the pace eventually slowed, I sat down to relax in a chair for the first time that day and looked out across the sea. The Bon festival was over, but soon the jellyfish would appear, so the crowds had come out while the swimming was still good.

Most people didn't go in the ocean, they just sat idly under an umbrella.

'They are mourning,' Nishino said later that night. 'They are mourning the summer that's gone by.'

I turned my gaze from the water back to the beach, where Nishino and Kikumi were sprawled next to each other under their umbrella. Kikumi had long legs. Recently she had found a lover. A woman, three years older, who worked in an office, apparently.

'I'm absolutely crazy about her,' Kikumi told me. We had been drinking barley tea at my apartment.

'Falling in love is nice,' Kikumi went on. 'To tell you the truth, I used to think that you and Nishino weren't really a good match, but now I can see that really isn't the case.' Kikumi started speaking faster as she neared the end of her speech. 'When you're in love, it barely makes any difference how old the person is or what kind of habits or nature they have.' Her lips were a shiny and glossy baby pink today.

Kikumi and Nishino looked like a father and daughter who got along well.

'That was so relaxing,' Nishino said that night. 'I really took it easy. Kikumi's a good kid. You have good people around you, Ai,' Nishino said solemnly. 'You create your own world, so that means that the person at the centre of it – you, Ai – you must be a really good kid too.' Nishino pulled gently on my hair.

'I don't really see it that way,' I replied brusquely.

*Nishino's so gloomy.* The thought flickered in my mind. Something about him had annoyed me. It was probably because I had worked all day without any rest. I soon closed my eyes and was half asleep. Beside me, I could sense Nishino propped up on his elbow, looking at my sleeping face. I rolled over. Nishino kept his gaze focused on my profile.


'He's probably crazy.'

As soon as the words were out of my mouth, they seemed to have an aura of certainty. Of course, everyone has a touch of madness in them. In fact, there's something frightening about a person who isn't a little crazy. But no matter how you looked at it, Nishino was definitely a deviant.

'Wasn't I the one who said that, a while back?' Nishino laughed as he spoke.

I picked up the thick chain that was attached to the

shackle around one of my ankles, and it made a rattling sound.

'So you don't run away, Ai,' Nishino had said when he put the shackle on me at the end of autumn. Of course, the key was in the top drawer of a bureau that was within reach of the chain.

'You can take it off any time you want to.' That was how Nishino had explained it.

'Why would you do such a thing?' I had asked. Nishino had lowered his gaze.

'Maybe to appal myself,' he had replied simply, after a brief pause.

As a result, I was now spending the majority of my time at Nishino's apartment. I read books or studied there. I listened to the radio or talked on the phone to Kikumi. It would have been easy to unchain myself, but for some reason I didn't feel the need to do so. I had the feeling that, the moment I were to take off the chain, Nishino was likely to start doing *really* eccentric things. As long as we both behaved collaboratively, it would be our little secret. But if one of us let it be known, then it would simply seem crazy.

'But isn't he crazy in a good way?' Kikumi said on the other end of the phone. 'For better or worse, love is full of madness,' she went on. Kikumi thought nothing more than that Nishino and I had practically shacked up together.

'Lucky you, Ai! I hope one day I'll have someone to live with like you do,' Kikumi murmured.

Nishino was very kind. These days, we hardly ever had sex.

'Do you know the novel called *The Collector*? Are we like that?' I had tried asking.

'No,' Nishino replied briefly, 'I have no interest in collecting.' Then he would undress me and slowly caress me, either my breasts or my back or my legs. I never wore underwear. Nishino's home was air-conditioned, and always at the perfect temperature.

'It's time for me to go home, you know.'

How many times did I come close to saying that? But I never did. I had the feeling I could leave him whenever I wanted.

'I love you,' Nishino would say.

'It's a simple enough thing, loving a girl,' Nishino went on quietly. 'I wonder why it is that I've never been able to love any of them.' And then he would embrace me in my stark nakedness.

I didn't love Nishino. I might not have even liked him. The thought of Nishino's death brought on not a single tear. I merely thought of it as an inevitability. Nishino embraced me tightly. He was crying. Why was this guy in tears? I wondered vaguely.

*Tomorrow – tomorrow for sure – I'll go home*, I would say to myself for the umpteenth time. But I knew that tomorrow would come and I would still be here. Within Nishino's home, I was like a small insect in hibernation, curled up and immobile.

Still, everything always comes to an end.

'Grapes,' Nishino had said. I had come down with a fever. It was a cold. A few days earlier, Nishino had started coughing, and he must have been contagious. Although

Nishino had no fever, and had been well enough to go off to work each day.

'I'll squeeze some grapes for you,' Nishino had said as he was going out of the front door. 'Some people say the best thing for a cold is tinned peaches, or sipping apple juice – but where I come from, it was always grapes,' Nishino had said cheerfully.

I had laughed. But laughing made me cough, which was painful.

'You take the skins off, take the seeds out too, and then squeeze all the juice out with a juicer. Back in the day, we didn't have a juicer though, so we'd use gauze to wring out all the juice. Oh, but that might not be good for a cough. It works for a fever, though. I don't know about a cough . . .' Nishino had muttered, as he bounded gaily out of the door, locking it behind him.

In my feverish, half-asleep state, I imagined the grapes. Large, deep purple orbs of fruit. In the garden of the house where I grew up, there was a grape arbour and, when summer arrived, so did the scarab beetles. Even though the grapes were still small and pale green, the scarab beetles would devour them messily. By the end of summer, there would only be a few clusters left uneaten by the insects. The grapes from the arbour bore sour fruit that had a tremendous number of seeds considering their small size.

*Maybe I really do love Nishino.* The thought occurred to me suddenly. No, no, that must just be the fever making me weak. I was dozing in and out of consciousness when the phone rang.

I had decided not to answer it, so I let it ring and heard

the answering machine pick up. 'No one is here to take your call,' the automated female voice said. I liked the voice on Nishino's answering machine just fine. I lay there, still, allowing the woman's voice to cover me like a blanket, when I heard Nishino on the machine.

'Ai.' He repeated my name several times.

I got up and staggered to the phone, unsteady on my feet.

'Is that you, Ai?' Nishino said.

'Um-hmm.'

'I'm sorry to bother you when you have a fever.'

'What's the matter?'

'I've had an accident.'

'Huh?'

'I don't think I'm going to make it.'

Nishino's voice carried the same upbeat tone that it had had earlier when he left the house. I thought he was joking.

'Ai, you never loved me, did you?' Nishino said on the other end of the line, sounding as happy as ever.

'That's not true,' I replied, without skipping a beat, before I even had a chance to think about it. As was my habit.

'It's all right. You and I are alike, Ai, so I understand.'

I murmured a response in my throat.

'Anyway, I'm waiting for the grapes,' I said, and went to hang up.

'Wait,' Nishino said. 'I wanted us to die together, but I guess there's nothing to be done about it. What a dull life mine has been, really, in the end.'

There was a click, and the line went dead. The sound of an ambulance's siren was coming from somewhere nearby. I collapsed back onto the bed, everything still a blur.

I could tell that my fever was raging. In my state between dreaming and waking, I became convinced that Nishino really was dead. I was utterly certain of it.

'I wanted to eat the grapes,' I murmured, and then I was drawn into a shallow yet insistent slumber.

*It's a good thing I'm not wearing the shackle today.* That was the last thing I remember thinking.

The funeral was absolutely magnificent. Many of his 'clients' came to burn offerings of incense, so it took a long time for the line of mourners to have their turn. Interspersed among them were several conspicuously attractive women.

The woman who had come to Enoshima with Nishino that time was there. And around her slim and lovely ankle, under her black stocking, she was still wearing the same gold chain.

'You're Ai, aren't you?' The woman from Enoshima spoke to me, when I was behind the temple, catching my breath after the incense lighting. She had a few more wrinkles than when I had seen her previously, but she was still beautiful.

'He's dead now, isn't he?' she kept speaking.

'You know who I am?' I asked, and the woman from Enoshima nodded.

'I saw him sometimes, and he told me about you.'

'Did you see him often?'

'Maybe once a month.'

'That's just like Nishino.' I laughed a little. He'd leave me in shackles, and then shrewdly go and meet up with his old girlfriend.

'But just for a meal,' the woman from Enoshima said, smiling. 'You never did love him, did you?' She peered into my eyes as she said this. I did not feel compelled to respond to such a question from someone I barely knew, and yet there was something about her I liked. For no good reason.

'Probably not,' I replied slowly.

'Serves him right,' the woman from Enoshima murmured. I remained silent.

'But you missed your chance, didn't you?' she went on.

'What?' I replied. 'Just what do you mean by that?'

'There may not have been much advantage in loving Nishino, but there were good times to be had, weren't there? It was hard work, worth doing,' the woman from Enoshima said, and then laughed out loud.

Her laugh was clear and pure. I myself was not laughing. I thought about the grapes.

I wondered what kind of grapes Nishino had planned to buy for me. Purple ones, or green ones? Would they have been the ones with small fruit? I wished he could have been able to spoon-feed me the cold, fresh-squeezed grape juice.

*Nishino*, I called out to him in my heart.

*Nishino, I never was able to love you. I'm sorry*, I said to him. I had the sense that I could hear Nishino sighing in my ear, but of course it was just my imagination.

'Thirty million years from now, they say there will be no more night.'

The woman from Enoshima looked shocked when these words came out of my mouth.

'Is that so?' she said, and then she turned her back on me.

'That's right,' I called out after the woman from Enoshima as she walked away.

That's right. Thirty million years from now, there will be no darkness in the world. Just what should I do, then? Tell me, what should I do?

# Mercury Thermometer

I'm going to try to talk about Nishino.

He was an odd kind of guy. Unlike anyone you had met before, or were likely to ever meet again. At the time, I had thought there would be others like him, but that wasn't the case. Nishino had said that I brought up a lot of memories for him, but now I am the one who remembers him wistfully. I wonder where he is and what he is doing. Is he still alive? No, he's probably dead by now, but vestiges of him remain indelible in my heart. And because of that, it makes no difference to me whether he is alive or dead.

Yukihiko Nishino. He was eighteen years old at the time. He had neither crimes nor accomplishments to his credit, nor any particular qualifications. Back then, his hobby was seeking out clay sewer pipes.

'You're Nozomi Misono, aren't you?'

This was the first thing Nishino ever said to me.

The voice came from directly above, and I opened my eyes slightly. My third lesson had been cancelled, so I had been lying on the grass in the rear courtyard by myself. The courtyard was shaded by jasmine bushes. It was the season when the bushes were covered with tiny pale yellow flowers, and it seemed like you only had to sit beside them briefly for their intoxicating fragrance to cling to you.

'I am – who are you?' I asked, as I sat up.

'Yukihiko Nishino. I'm a first-year student in the economics department.'

'I see,' I said, staring at Nishino. He had neatly trimmed, brownish hair that didn't have any wave. He had on jeans and a white T-shirt, over which he wore a long-sleeved blue denim shirt that was undone to the third button.

I didn't recognize him. I only knew two guys who were in the economics department, and both of them were third-year students like me.

'I'm not a suspicious character,' Nishino said, seeming to widen his eyes.

'But isn't it suspicious to use the phrase "suspicious character" in the first place?' I asked in reply, laughing. Nishino laughed too.

'I was behind you in secondary school.'

'Ah.' I nodded.

Back in secondary school, I had been president of the student council. At the time, it was unusual for a girl to be president, and though it had been three years since graduation, even now whenever I went back home, students I had gone to school with – familiar and unfamiliar faces, both – would still regularly come up and speak to me.

'So . . . ?'

I may have been a sort of local 'celebrity' back home, but having come to Tokyo for university, I was just another student in the crowd. I had decided to run for president out of sheer curiosity – I thought I might want to know what it would be like to run the student council. But, as it turned out, I received an unprecedented percentage of the votes. Mind you, this was a time and a place where being female still had a certain significance. And so, ever since, I had become a 'school superstar'.

Entering university had finally freed me from that uncomfortable role. With this aim, I had paid careful and deliberate attention to choosing a mid-size 'vanilla' university that most people in my town hadn't heard of. And I had hit the mark – since enrolling at this college, I had yet to meet a single person from my secondary school.

'I know this may seem like a rude question, but is it true that you'll have sex with anyone, Misono?'

Nishino's eyes opened even wider as he asked me this. At this point in time, I did not yet know that Nishino had a habit of opening his eyes wide when he was being dead serious, that there was nothing frivolous about this exchange.

'Your question may be rude, but it's just as rude to eyeball someone like that – didn't your mother teach you?' I said, and with the rigid spine of *Exercises in Thermodynamics I* that was in my hand, I gave Nishino's shin a good hard knock.

'Yow!' Nishino yelped and crouched down. The jasmine bushes swayed, and several of the flowers scattered. I stood up slowly, brushed the grass off me and, without another glance at Nishino, I walked away.

*

The next time I saw Nishino was about a month later.

He was walking beside a girl on the path towards the literature department building. *She must not be a student at our college*, I thought to myself.

The reason is, the girl was pretty. Of course, there were plenty of pretty girls at our college. Just as our college held a mid-size ranking, so the prettiness of its female students was also somehow 'mid-size'.

But the prettiness of the girl next to Nishino far surpassed 'mid-size' – her looks were exceptional. She was clearly and undeniably pretty.

I would have bet that this pretty girl was a long-term veteran of trading on her good looks. That is to say, with regard to her own prettiness, she had not the slightest doubt.

'Hey.' Nishino waved at me.

'Hey,' I said in return. I did not make it a practice to have anything to do with guys who ask rude questions – my interest was merely piqued by his obvious talent for getting a girl of such calibre to come all the way over to another university's campus.

'Hello.' The girl next to Nishino bowed her head. Nishino's attitude was laid-back. Their demeanour was like that of a couple who had been married for years.

'Your girlfriend?' I asked.

'Yeah,' Nishino admitted freely. 'This is Kanoko, dear,' Nishino went on.

'Don't call me "dear",' she said to Nishino, her cheerful voice expressing regret as she cast a smile in my direction with just the right amount of courtesy.

*That was a mistake*, I thought to myself. I should have immediately pretended I didn't know him and run off.

'Misono. Well, see you,' I spun on my heel and tried to walk away. Nishino was placid as ever.

'Oh,' said 'Kanoko, dear'.

Doing my best not to turn around, I glanced over from just the corner of my eye.

'Kanoko, dear' was mystified. Surprisingly, she had taken notice that I was annoyed by the prospect of having to spend any more time in their presence. And what was even more surprising was that 'Kanoko, dear' seemed apologetic about it.

Now, unable to coolly take my leave, I stood frozen in this in-between position.

'It was a pleasure to meet you,' said 'Kanoko, dear' after a brief hesitation.

'Yeah,' I replied, with my back still half turned.

'Kanoko, dear' seemed to soften a bit at the tone of my voice.

I have at times wondered just what guys make of this sort of 'psychological power struggle' between women, which can resemble foreign diplomacy in its subtleties. Most guys probably don't even notice it. In fact, it's unlikely they grasp the idea that such a thing even exists.

Sure enough, Nishino simply stood there, with nothing more than a fresh-faced smile.

This time I turned all the way around, so that they were now behind me.

'Should we go?' I heard Nishino say. 'Kanoko, dear' didn't reply, but I heard the sound of both of their footsteps and I could tell that they were walking away in sync.

I hurried towards the science department building on the edge of campus.

For a long time after that, I didn't happen to run into Nishino. If things had gone on that way, I might never have given him a second thought.

But there was the matter of the clay sewer pipes. The reason I encountered Nishino again was the clay sewer pipes.

It had been a busy week. Monday, I had been with Minakawa. Tuesday, I spent the afternoon with Suzuki, the evening with Kaneko and, when I got back to my place after midnight, Munakata came over. Wednesday and Thursday, I was stuck in the lab until late so I was on my own, but Friday and Saturday, I stayed over at Nakajima's place.

Of course, I was having sex with each of these guys.

I couldn't say whether having sex with five different guys in one week was far outside of the ordinary or whether it was actually surprisingly common. Only that, the answer to the question Nishino had asked me, 'Will you have sex with anyone?' was no.

I didn't have sex with just anyone. I've never once had sex with a guy I didn't find interesting. When I have sex with someone, it always comes down to pure curiosity. Exactly like when I was in secondary school and decided to run for president of the student council.

So that was how, that week in particular, I came to share various intimate moments with five different guys. That's what I like about having sex with a guy – being able to have these intimate moments. The guy gets used to me. He starts to express a certain affection. He forgets his manners somewhat. His character simplifies. And, if things go well, he falls in love with me.

Sunday, I spent the day by myself. I considered Sunday my Sabbath day. I did laundry, I tidied up, I cooked, I watched television – either the broadcast of a baseball game or a marathon or, if it was the season for sumo, I would leave that on. I may have had an insatiable curiosity, but spending time with people around the clock was exhausting.

When evening fell, I went to the park in my neighbourhood. This park was vast. One section of it was reserved for children's playground equipment, while another sizable part had been left as fields.

I always walked over to the part that was fields. I would stand among the weeds that tickled my ankles, and stare at the swings or the slide. At that time of day, there were never any people in the park. The swings swayed in the breeze. The chains made a creaking sound. The grasses at my feet rustled.

From time to time, I would crawl into a clay sewer pipe. Near a spot in the field where the grass grew especially dense, there were several weather-beaten clay sewer pipes. They were each at least a metre in diameter. The first time I saw them, I had thought, *I bet it's relaxing to crawl inside*, and then I promptly crawled into one of them. I know I'm repeating myself, but I like to obey my curiosity.

That Sunday too, I was inside a clay sewer pipe. I was sitting with my back leaning up against the curve, with a photo album I had brought with me open, gazing at the black and white photographs. I had climbed in further than usual, so it was dark. The page I had had open for a while showed a beach with dozens of cats. This photograph had the highest contrast between dark and light, and so it was easy to see, even in the murky twilight.

At some point I must have fallen asleep.

'Is that you, Misono?' Hearing this voice, I sat up with a start. Doing so, I bumped my head against the wall of the pipe.

'Yow!' I cried out.

'Oh, sorry,' said the voice of the speaker. 'Though I guess that makes us even,' the voice went on. As I rubbed my head, I looked towards the opening, where the speaker had stooped down and was trying to come inside. I could not see his face in the backlight. But I had a pretty good guess who it was.

The speaker, his voice tidy and lacking any edge, was none other than Nishino.


'It's really nice in here, isn't it?' Nishino said, from right beside me.

The sun had almost completely set. My eyes had grown accustomed to the darkness and I could clearly make out Nishino's silhouette, but for him, having just crawled inside, it must have been practically pitch dark. As he groped his way along, Nishino came to lean up against the curve.

'I like clay sewer pipes too. I often spend my Sundays going around looking for them,' Nishino said.

'You mean you've liked clay sewer pipes for a long time?' I asked with surprise. 'You're an oddball.'

We were right up beside each other. I could feel the warmth from Nishino's body. Even with the two of us there, it was still very relaxing. Just like when I was alone. It didn't feel like I was in there with a stranger. It reminded me a bit of when you're in the midst of having sex.

'Sorry about that, before,' Nishino said, as he peered at my face. His eyes seemed quite well adjusted to the darkness. His fingers suddenly touched my fringe.

'Before what?'

'For asking that strange question.'

'That strange question aside,' I replied, 'what seemed weird to me was that you – someone I had never met before – would presume to know anything about my sex life.'

'I heard it from Minakawa.'

'Is that right?' I said. Minakawa was the guy from last Monday. Or was it Tuesday? I couldn't remember exactly. He was one of the two guys I knew who were in the economics department. I had always suspected Minakawa of being a little on the careless side, and it turned out I had been right.

'But still, why did you seek me out to ask me that question for yourself?' I asked after a few moments of silence.

'I wanted to know,' Nishino replied. His eyes were wide open. He wore the same expression as when he had first asked me that question.

'What was it you wanted to know?'

'How can you love someone?'

'What?' I sputtered. Of all the things to ask, inside a clay sewer pipe! Only what might be the most important question in life. Just who was this guy?

Amidst my surprise, I started to hiccup. My hiccups went on, several times fiercely, and then more softly, every few seconds, like a geyser.

'They won't stop,' Nishino said, holding back his laughter.

'Nope, they won't stop,' I replied, in between hiccups.

'Shall we stop them?'

No sooner had he said this than Nishino lifted my chin and brought his lips in close. His tongue probed deeply around the inside of my mouth.

For the next few moments, Nishino tried this and that.

'But they still haven't stopped, have they?' I exclaimed, once Nishino let go of my face. Nishino puffed out his cheeks.

'I guess I'm no good after all,' he said. 'I can't even stop a single hiccup.' His tone was terribly sad. At first I thought he was kidding but, on the contrary, he seemed to be speaking with unexpected seriousness.

'You're too much,' I laughed, as I tapped Nishino on his puffed-up cheeks.

I realized that, just this moment, I had developed a tremendous curiosity about this guy.

'Wanna come over tonight?' I asked swiftly.

'Sure,' Nishino said. We crawled towards the opening. Once we were outside, we saw that it was completely dark. At some point, my hiccups had stopped without my noticing.


Nishino and I did not have sex that day.

I made dinner for Nishino. I cooked ham and eggs to go with the potatoes I had boiled earlier in the day. I also served miso soup with tofu. I may have unconsciously avoided sex since Sunday was, after all, my Sabbath day.

Instead, I got to hear Nishino's life story.

'I'm aware of how unusual it is to have this kind of

conversation with a woman I've practically only just met.' Nishino prefaced his story with this statement.

'But we haven't just met,' I said. Nishino nodded, opening his eyes wide.

'I know,' he said. 'But as far as you're concerned, Misono, you barely know me. It's just that . . .'

Nishino broke off there and tilted his head.

*He's a strange guy*, I thought to myself. I was intrigued. Something about him didn't add up.

'It's just that, to me, it doesn't feel as though we've just met. You seem close already, like an old friend I've known a long time,' Nishino went on softly.

'What?' I sputtered again. 'We might have shared something in the clay sewer pipe, but how can you just go off into your own world like that?'

'Oh, I see, sorry,' Nishino apologized in a mild tone. 'It's just that you – Nozomi Misono – you bring up a lot of memories for me. I mean, it's not you yourself who I remember, and you're absolutely right that it's all very sudden. But still . . .'

And with that 'But still . . .' Nishino told me a story, the gist of which I'll recount here.


Nishino had had a sister, twelve years older than him.

When Nishino was in primary school, his sister got married.

A few years later, his sister gave birth to a little girl.

Six months after that, the little girl died suddenly of congenital heart disease.

His sister's marriage, which had never been a happy one, worsened.

After the child's death, his sister's physical condition deteriorated.

His sister had moved back to her parents' home.

Three years ago, the summer after the spring when Nishino had started secondary school, his sister killed herself.

Ever since then, Nishino had been wracked with guilt and regret over all the things he couldn't do for his sister, and had begun to suspect that he might have been in love with her.

And I – Nozomi Misono – looked exactly like his sister.

'Is that so?' I said cautiously, after listening to his story.

I never would have imagined that, beneath the veneer of his unblemished skin and vigorously healthy musculature, Nishino harboured a secret like this story.

Nishino relayed all this as he voraciously ate the ham and four sunny-side-up eggs that I had made at his request. Nishino seemed so frank and open about it, I found myself wondering if he might be joking.

'That must have been awful,' I said with even more caution.

Counselling services fell outside my area of speciality. It goes without saying that this applied to general matters of incest as well.

'Hey, so do you wanna, maybe, have sex?'

I had ventured this question because, after telling his story, Nishino had seemed quite indifferent. So indifferent, in fact, that maybe I found it a bit disturbing.

'No, I can't have sex with you, Misono. Not now, at least. Like I said, I'm still trying to figure out whether or not I wanted to sleep with my sister,' Nishino replied with all seriousness.

*I'm not your sister.* I thought about saying this to him, but I chose not to.

Nishino had picked up an apple that was in a basket on the dining table, and he spun it around in his hands.

'Shall I peel the apple?' I asked, and Nishino said yes.

'Um, it would be nice if you could make rabbit ears,' Nishino went on. 'You know, peel the skin in the shape of floppy rabbit ears.'

'Sure. Though I'll probably mess them up,' I replied. Nishino seemed to enjoy watching the knife in my hand.

'My sister used to make rabbits for me a lot,' Nishino said with a laugh.

'Huh?' I drew in my breath, and Nishino opened his eyes wide.

'No, I'm perfectly aware of what's going on. I don't have any suspicious intentions.'

I waited a beat, and then I replied with deliberate cheer, 'You know, the fact that you said that in the first place is suspicious.'

In that moment of comic relief after breaking the tension, I almost dropped the knife. I held the knife more tightly, trying not to let Nishino notice, and fashioned two rabbits, which I set down in front of Nishino. I peeled the remaining two pieces of apple the normal way, and ate those myself.

For a while, the sound of us munching on the apple slices filled the room.

*

'But why?' Nishino asked.

Nishino had sex with me the next day, after all. Still saying something about how he couldn't do it, 'Not now, at least.'

Nishino had been lingering in my apartment for too long, and I hadn't managed to figure out how to drive him away, so I finally gave in and let him stay over. Despite the fact that I had previously decided that only Munakata was allowed to sleep over – figuring that since he had a wife and kid, he wouldn't make it a habit.

Nishino's sex drive was as voracious as his appetite.

Munakata liked to say that twenty-year-old guys were all at their peak and always good-to-go but, actually, there was tremendous variation among them. Some guys were like Nishino, keen to express their desire, while some didn't seem to want much sex at all. But among this horde, Nishino's sex drive was superior. Nishino's sexual appetite had a certain tenacity that the others lacked.

Having sexual tenacity doesn't always translate into good sex, but having sex with Nishino was, in fact, good.

*This guy might really turn out to be somebody*, I had thought idly to myself. But just what kind of somebody? I chuckled a bit at this interior monologue.

'What are you laughing about?' Nishino asked.

'Nothing at all,' I replied, but Nishino seemed discontent. In this regard, he was no different from every other guy.

'Why do you have to sleep with so many guys, Nozomi?' Finally spent, Nishino had posed this question slowly, having pulled the quilt up under his chin and assumed an excellent position for dozing off.

'You're one to talk – how are things with Kanoko, dear?' I tossed the question back at him.

'Oh, right,' Nishino said with a note of surprise. 'Now that you mention it, I guess maybe this could be considered two-timing.'

'Don't say stupid things,' I replied, furrowing my brow. I might have laughed as well but, for some reason, I couldn't bring myself to smile. Because I knew that Nishino's surprise had been genuine. Just this once, Nishino had completely forgotten about 'Kanoko, dear'.

'We're not close enough to each other for this to be considered two-timing,' I said dismissively. 'Kanoko, dear' weighed on my mind. I certainly didn't hate her. No, it wasn't her. If there was anyone I hated, it was likely to be Nishino.

'But, Nozomi, I wish I had more with you,' Nishino said.

'If there was anything between us,' I said flatly.

I had remembered Nishino's question, How can you love someone? I cursed him in my mind – how could he ask that, when he was the one so easily capable of love?

*When he is so easily capable of anything*, I thought. Right at that moment, I was sick of Nishino, all neat and tidy. I was completely sick of his good sex too, for that matter. Get out of here, I was about to say. But I didn't say it, of course. Because I knew very well that my frustration with Nishino was nothing more than frustration with my own self.

Nishino was cool. But his coolness was lined with warmth. That's what was difficult to reconcile. How was it any different from me, with my pretence of loving every guy I intended to have sex with, when it was more likely that I didn't love any of them. I knew these things were one and the same.

'Your sister would be sad,' I said.

Nishino turned pale. 'Nozomi, you're mean,' he murmured.

'You're right,' I replied with a grin.

Nishino got dressed and left. I didn't hear from him for a long time after that.


One by one, I replaced my sexual partners.

Minakawa was out – having confirmed his carelessness, I was the one who put distance between us – then Kaneko graduated and we drifted apart. Munakata was busy with work, so Hakozaki, Taisho and Nozue took their places. Once Nekoda and Minakata joined the line-up, I now had the highest-ever number of 'boys I loved', and by the time I started my fourth year, my roster was in good working order.

I was forthright about having multiple lovers with some of my partners, but there were others who were uninformed – although they may have had their suspicions. The decision whether or not to tell each of them depended on their temperament and disposition.

Among the ones I determined it was okay to tell, not a single one demonstrated a strong opposition to me dating anyone other than himself. Perhaps this indicated a lack of attachment to me on their part, or else an uninhibited and free-thinking spirit – I wasn't sure which – but I could say, at the very least, that my ability to judge people was quite impressive. Though it might also be fair to say that Minakawa, who had disenchanted me with his carelessness, had been a slight miscalculation.

I had been passing the days like this, without incident. I had practically forgotten about Nishino. Which is why I was surprised when I ran into him, about a year after that day when he and I had had sex.

We bumped into each other in the unisex toilets of an *izakaya* near our university.

'Nozomi, I don't know what it is, but I feel so empty,' Nishino said as soon as he saw me. The tone of his voice implied that we had just seen each other the day before.

He was, as always, the kind of guy who was easily lost in his own world.

'Do you really,' I replied coolly.

Nishino was quite drunk. His breath reeked of alcohol.

'I'm such a lightweight,' Nishino mumbled, and the next moment, without hesitation – I didn't even have a chance to dodge him – he kissed me, right in front of the sink.

'Quick, let's make our getaway,' Nishino said, a string of saliva trailing from the corner of his mouth. It was silky and transparent.

'No way,' I replied.

'Well then, be my girlfriend instead.'

'You say "instead", but isn't running away together and being your girlfriend exactly the same thing?'

'I guess you're right,' Nishino said, opening his eyes wide. He thought about it for another moment.

Ready to be done with this sloppy drunk and go back to my seat, I turned my back on Nishino. The instant I did so, to my surprise, he burst into audible sobs.

*

'Waah,' Nishino cried.

Nishino cried his heart out. It was not the typical crying of a male university student. It was more like that of a five-year-old child.

'Nozomi, I'm so sad,' Nishino stammered through his tears.

'You've got to stop,' I muttered. But, of course, my words didn't reach Nishino. He was too busy crying.

'Tell me, how come this world is so relentless?' Nishino asked.

'Who knows?' I replied. Those words too were lost on Nishino, drowned out by his sobs.

'I can't take it any more, the relentlessness.'

'I know,' I responded gently. I supposed it was the least I could do.

'Nozomi, you're going to be a scientist, aren't you? So then, can't you explain to me why this world is the way that it is?'

'I'm probably not going to be a scientist. I'm probably not good enough.'

'So then, the world will just keep on going, ceaselessly.'

'Yeah,' I said. 'The world really is endless. But that's because, in the beginning, there was the Big Bang and, ever since then, the universe has continued to expand, and there's nothing we can do about it, right?' I responded with seriousness, in an attempt to comfort Nishino.

'The universe, you say it's expanding?' Nishino asked, his eyes opening wide.

'That's what I've been told.'

'So then, what's on the other side of the expanding universe?'

'The other side?'

'Yeah. On the outermost edge of the expansion, further beyond, where it's not yet the universe.'

I was at a loss for words. This thought had never occurred to me. The thing that was in the empty space outside this universe? Was that a void? But could there really be a void on the other side of this universe? And just what did that mean anyway, a 'void'?

'There's definitely nothing on the other side,' I replied, at last.

'There's nothing on the other side. Nothing whatsoever.' I faced Nishino with heartfelt solemnity. He would have been devastated unless I addressed him with the same level of gravity as if I were consoling an overwrought five-year-old child.

'I see. So you mean, the randomness is because there's nothing on the other side?' Nishino said quietly, after a slight pause. His voice finally sounded like his own. He wasn't even crying any more.

'Nozomi, I'm sorry,' Nishino said after another moment of silence. 'It's been a long time since I cried. Maybe since my sister died.'

In spite of myself, my own tears welled up the instant I heard him say these words. Nishino's crying must have been contagious.

'No way,' I said, as I turned away from Nishino. Without looking back, I walked out of the unisex toilets.

When I got back to where I was sitting, the boys from my class were singing a dirty song. With a sigh, I poured some saké into my cup. I let out several more sighs as I took small sips of the heated saké that had now cooled.

I only saw Nishino once more after that. It was the day before I graduated.

Since my place happened to be conveniently located for the commute to my new job, I was spared the need to find a new apartment and, without much sympathy for my hustling and bustling classmates, I passed the days idly.

There was a light knock on the door. Suspicious, since there was an intercom, I left the chain on the door and opened it a crack.

'Hey,' Nishino said through the narrow gap of the open door.

'Hey,' I replied, unlatching the chain.

Nishino came into the apartment with a nonchalant manner. If there are a thousand different variations on the way a guy might enter a girl's apartment, there are far more deviations when the guy has already had sex with the girl.

Nishino's entry was neither overly familiar nor overly guarded – he hit just the right note.

*Damn, this guy really could turn out to be somebody*, I thought to myself.

'Look, this is for you,' Nishino said, and from his pocket he pulled out something that gleamed, thin and silvery.

'A thermometer?'

What Nishino held in the palm of his hand was an

old-fashioned tube with a light blue cap, inside which was a mercury thermometer.

'Yeah. It was my sister's.'

'What?' I gasped. 'I can't accept something like that,' I said reflexively.

'I guess it's kind of creepy,' Nishino said with a laugh.

'Yeah, it's creepy,' I bluntly agreed.

'But I've been using it ever since my sister died,' Nishino stated with an odd reasoning.

'That makes it even creepier,' I said.

Nishino scratched his head. 'So you don't want it? Even though my temperature replaced hers?'

'There you are, still immersed in your own world.'

Nishino laughed heartily at what I had said. Things seemed somewhat uncertain. Why had Nishino showed up at this odd moment to bring me this odd thing?

Then we had dinner together – leftover curry from earlier in the day – and we parted without having sex.


That represents the entirety of how I knew Nishino.

Every so often, I still think back on what a strange guy he was. I never really knew him all that well. And yet, I'm left with the sense that we were quite close. We shared a certain sensitivity. But also, at times, an utter insensitivity.

It has occurred to me that children might be like that too. Come to think of it, on the day I met Nishino in the clay sewer pipe, that night as he was drifting off to sleep Nishino had said, 'I wish that my sister had had a son instead of a daughter.' When I asked him why, Nishino was silent for a moment, and then he replied, 'Because then I could have been reincarnated in his place.'

'My goodness – Nishino, you were already born, you were already growing up, weren't you? That's not how reincarnation works,' I had said.

Nishino had pursed his lips and argued, 'But at least then it would be easier for me to project myself onto him.'

The next morning, I was brushing my teeth when Nishino came up behind me and said, 'I've changed my mind.'

'About what?' I asked, my mouth full of toothpaste and the toothbrush.

'Since there's nothing I can do about the dead, I'm not going to obsess about the past. Instead, from now on I'm going to become my sister, and give birth to a baby girl,' he said.

'That makes even less sense,' I said dismissively. Nishino hung his head.

'Well, I just can't accept it,' he said, drooping even lower. The reason why, ultimately, I ended up having sex with Nishino may have been the way he hung his head then.

I never heard anything else about Nishino. As for the mercury thermometer, he pressed it on me until eventually I accepted it. Every so often, just to see, I take my temperature. Most of the time it's normal.

After I've taken my temperature, when I shake it with a hard flick of my wrist to bring the mercury back down, the thermometer makes a faint sound as it cuts through the air. Whenever I hear that sound, I can't help but think about Nishino's life.

I wonder if someday, somewhere, Nishino was ever able to meet his sister and her child again.

Did he ever learn what is on the other side of the expanding universe?

Was he able to live out his life, and to love someone?

Did he ever find a place for himself in this relentless world?